TENDERNESS

TENDERNESS

Robert Cormier

VICTOR GOLLANCZ
LONDON

First published in Great Britain 1997
by Victor Gollancz
An imprint of the Cassell Group
Wellington House, 125 Strand, London WC2R 0BB

A catalogue record for this book is
available from the British Library

ISBN 0 575 06433 1

Typeset by CentraCet, Cambridge
Printed in Great Britain by St Edmundsbury Press Ltd,
Bury St Edmunds, Suffolk

97 98 99   5 4 3 2 1

In memory of the teachers
who changed the course of my life:

Sister Catherine
E. Lillian Ricker
Florence D. Conlon

To know the pain of too much tenderness.
             —*Kahlil Gibran*

A part of the body that has been injured
is often tender to the touch.

PART I

Me, I get fixated on something and I can't help myself. Sometimes it's nice and I let myself drift to see what will happen. Like with Throb. Sometimes it's not so nice, but I still have to go with it and can do nothing to stop. That's the scary part, when it's not nice at all. But even when it's nice, it's scary. Anything that takes over your life is scary, although there can be pleasure in it.

With Throb, it was nice in the beginning, the music, and his voice on the CDs and, of course, the words, and the way he sang them, his voice rough, like gravel in his throat but the words, thrilling:

> *Pluck my heart*
> *From my flesh*
> *And eat it . . .*

Dark music, I call it. Music that speaks to me. Dark and black from the pits of night:

> *Call my name*
> *From the grave*
> *Of your rotting love*

11

I had to listen hard to make out the words, closing my eyes, pressing the earphones tight against my ears, thinking at first that he sang *rotten love* instead of *rotting love*, which is another thing altogether.

Anyway, it was nice sitting in the library next to the CD player, the earphones on, people coming and going at the circulation desk and me listening, like on a private island in the middle of all that activity, and I would close my eyes and listen to him, his voice filling my ears and the inside of my head:

A hole in my mouth
To match the hole in my heart
Through which your love howls

I didn't get fixated on Throb until I saw the actual hole in his mouth on *Entertainment Tonight*, the missing tooth, his spiky hair the colour of salmon, his freckles and that terrible clown outfit: baggy pants and no shirt, his nipples like old pennies stuck on his chest. But most of all that missing tooth, like a black cave in his mouth. And that was when I got fixated on him, staring at the black cave and knowing that I had to press my lips against his lips and put my tongue through that hole in his mouth.

I stole the CD at Aud-Vid Land at the mall even though the CD player at home is broken, like everything else in the place. I didn't exactly steal the CD, which would be imposs-ible because of the security gate, but I didn't pay for it, either. There's this guy, the assistant manager, who's like forty years old, and he opens the door of the stockroom and I slip inside and wait for him. He likes to look at me. I close my eyes. He tells me to stand this way, then that way. I hear him breathing. Finally, he says, "Okay." I open my eyes but do not enjoy looking at him. His complexion is terrible, and he wears bright yellow socks.

At home I remove the CD and look at Throb's face spread across the entire booklet, which opens out like an accordion. I Scotch-tape it to the wall, after taking down the picture of me and my mother posing in front of the Lincoln Memorial in Washington, DC. Lincoln is my favourite president. I feel bad for him because he looks so depressed all the time and his face is on the penny, the cheapest coin of all.

Gary watches me from the doorway.

"Lori," he says. "Your mother's gonna feel bad, taking that picture down."

"I'll put it up someplace else," I tell him, stepping back to look at Throb there on my wall, with the hole in his mouth.

Gary's not like some of the others my mother brings home. He's been with us for, like, six months. He doesn't use bad language and he works steady, the night shift at Murdock's Tool and Die. He drinks too much sometimes, which makes him fall asleep all over the place, which is a nice change from Dexter, who got mean and nasty when he drank and hit my mother once in a while.

Gary looks at me as I look at Throb's picture. I can *feel* him looking at me, something he's been doing lately. He also rubs close to me when he meets me in the hallway on the way to the bathroom. It's nice to have him look at me like that but I don't want to do anything to hurt my mother, even though she's a pain in the ass sometimes. She has enough problems. She was always a beauty but lately she seems to be fading right before my eyes. I see the grooves in her face where her make-up cakes, and the eye-drops don't always obliterate the red anymore. She's also beginning to sag. I caught sight of her getting out of the shower one night and was surprised to see her drooping. She was always proud of her figure and says that was her best gift to me, a good figure, although we both have to worry about gaining weight and I am sometimes embarrassed by how big I am on top.

Gary comes and stands beside me in front of the picture. We are alone in the house, my mother at work for the lunch-time rush at Timson's. It's hot, early June, and heat seems to be radiating out of him, his arm pressing against my arm and the perspiration, like, gluing us together. I hear his sharp intake of breath, or maybe it's my own. Suddenly his arm is around me and he's caressing me on top and I lean against him. His aftershave lotion is sharp and spicy in my nostrils and his hand feels good, tender, and I want him to continue but I pull away from him, thinking of my mother.

He removes his hand and says, "S-Sorry," stammering a bit, and I don't say anything, just stand there feeling depressed. I feel depressed because I know that if Gary stays—and my mother wants him to stay, permanently, maybe—then I have to leave. Again.

The next day I read in the newspaper that Throb will be appearing this weekend at the ConCentre in Wickburg, where we used to live, and my fixation intensifies. Wickburg is down in Massachusetts, about a hundred miles from this stupid little town where we've been living for a year and a half, and I'm convinced that Wickburg is my destination and my fate and the place where I will put my tongue in the black hole in Throb's mouth, leaving Gary and my mother to live happily ever after.

Happily ever after sounds like a fairy tale but my mother believes in fairy tales, happy endings and rainbows. She always thinks tomorrow will be better than today, and believes only the good weather forecasts, never the bad. She drives me crazy repeating stuff, like if you get handed a lemon, make lemonade, or it's always darkest just before the dawn. Once, early in the morning, rain pelting the windows, she sat at the kitchen table, pressing an ice bag against a black eye she received from Dexter. She looked up brightly from the newspaper on the table and said, "Listen to this, Lori, my horoscope: 'Brightness everywhere, keep up the good work, your talents will be recognized.' Isn't that grand?"

The ice bag slipped down a bit and I saw the bruise, ugly and purple, near her eye.

"What's the matter?" she asked. "You look as if you're going to cry."

"I think I'm coming down with a cold," I said. But I wasn't coming down with a cold.

My mother is a waitress. A professional, proud of it. Always shows up on time, whether she has a hangover or not. Knows the proper way to hold a tray above her shoulder. Knows when the customer wants the check, whether the soup is not hot enough or the steak well done and not medium as requested.

She has bad luck with men. Always picks the wrong guy except in one or two cases, like Gary, for instance, and my father, who she says was kind and gentle but without any luck at all, hit by a car on a rainy night when I was two years old. I don't remember him at all. I have never seen a picture of him, not even a wedding picture. "It all happened on the run," my mother said. Which is the way things always happen with her.

On the run. Maybe that's the story of my mother's life and

mine, too. Moving from place to place all the time. Always looking for a better job or following somebody she met who makes promises that are always broken. Like Dexter Campbell, who she followed from Wickburg to Portsmouth, New Hampshire, where he abandoned her while she was in the hospital. She went to the hospital emergency room after he beat her up that time. I sat with her in the waiting room watching the small lump on her forehead actually grow to the size of an egg. She told the doctor she walked into a door after getting up to go to the bathroom in the middle of the night.

"How about this?" the doctor asked, pointing to the bruise on her arm.

"I bruise easy," my mother said. "My skin is sensitive."

The doctor looked at me and I looked away.

"Are you all right?" he asked, touching my shoulder with a gentle hand.

I nodded. Dexter never touched me. Touched my mother, his hands everywhere and half-undressing her and himself, too, in front of me while my mother whispered, "Not here, not in front of the kid," but he went on anyway.

Anyway, Dexter was gone when we returned from the hospital. My mother said, "He was afraid, the bastard, that I was going to turn him in." The apartment belonged to Dexter, rent was paid for the next month, but we left anyway, caught a bus to Manchester, where my mother knew someone who ran an all-night diner and would give her a job maybe. Then from Manchester to this town, my mother apologizing all over the place as usual for making us move so much, changing schools.

"Lucky you're so smart," she says all the time. "Smarter than your dumb mother . . ."

"You're not so dumb," I tell her. "You're a very good waitress. You never get fired. You always quit . . ."

"I worry about you." My mother says this all the time, too. Last week she said it again and added, "Look at you, fifteen years old. I can't believe it . . ."

What she means is that she can't believe she's thirty-six.

"I always think of myself first," she says. "I'm not a very good mother, Lori."

"You're a very good mother," I tell her. It doesn't cost anything to say that, and it makes her feel good.

"I wonder what will happen to you in that terrible world out there," she says. Her optimism deserts her now and then, when there's nothing to drink in the house and no money to buy any.

She doesn't know, of course, what has already happened to me. She still thinks I am a virgin and I guess I am. Technically, that is. I mean, I have had my moments with boys in the rear seats at Cinema I and II at the mall, and in the back seats of cars and with some others, like the CD guy, but never all the way.

I have been trying to figure out what love is and the difference between sex and love and that other thing, lust. I think one of my teachers was in love with me, but he never touched me. Mr Sinclair. He told me that I had a beautiful spirit, that I had a talent for writing and should keep a journal, and his eyes on me made my legs quiver, all that longing in his eyes and maybe sadness, too. I used to linger after school outside his classroom. He discovered me there one afternoon as he came through the doorway and we almost bumped into each other. He broke into a smile but stepped back right away, the smile wiped away like erasing a scribble on a blackboard, and he looked worried and concerned, glancing around.

"Hi, Mr Sinclair," I said, so glad to be with him alone in the corridor, my heart dancing.

He was not handsome, eyes deep in their sockets, hair always askew, harsh lines in his cheeks. I always wondered whether he got enough sleep.

He blushed and coughed there in the corridor, slapping his briefcase against his hip and stammering something I couldn't understand. But I saw the longing in his eyes and the pain there, too.

"Oh, Lorelei," he said, saying that name I hated—I was named after my mother's favourite aunt—thank God for nicknames.

I wanted to take his hand and place it on me and tell him not to be afraid, but instead we just looked at each other, and he turned away from me, looking at me over his shoulder, such sadness in his eyes, still looking at me as he turned the corner, taking with him all my longings and maybe his longings, too.

I wondered again what those longings were.

Yet what I think I want most of all is someone who would be tender with me.

Mr Sinclair once asked the class to make a list of the ten most beautiful words in the English language, and the only word that really seemed beautiful to me was *tenderness*.

I am on my way. With my backpack and Reeboks and my cut-off jeans. It's a beautiful June morning, everything green by the roadside. The bus from Hookset to Garville dropped me near Route 2, and I am standing by the side of the road hitching to Wickburg. I have hitched all over the place. Times I got mad at my mother, I would take off and hitch someplace. Like taking a lottery ticket. I always dreamed of a great-looking guy stopping and picking me up and telling me he's heading for California via the Rocky Mountains and I say let's go and he's also kind and gentle and we drive all over the USA through small towns and big cities. But it never happens that way.

There's a pause between passing cars, the highway empty, and the whole world seems empty suddenly and I want to go home and have Gary be tender with me. Or somebody.

Forget it, I tell myself.

I left my mother a note. Not a long one. *Going away for a while, Mom. Don't worry. I'll be staying with my friends in Wickburg, Martha and George.* There are no friends in Wickburg. I made them up. She actually believes they exist, that I visit them when I take off. I wonder if she only pretends to believe and this eases her conscience for letting me go and not calling the cops to find me. Or is it cruel to think of her like that? Anyway, I pretend that I receive letters from Martha and George. She never sees the letters, of course, because there are no letters. I pick a day when she's not at home at the time the mail arrives. When she arrives home and asks, "Any good mail today?" (meaning letters without windows, because windows mean bills), I tell her, "Yes, Martha wrote to me." And my mother drifts away, looking for a drink as she always does when she arrives home, either from work or shopping or maybe a walk around the block. She has never connected my friends with Martha and George Washington.

I left the note where she will find it easily. I am glad this time that she won't be alone, that she has Gary with her now.

I am always careful when I hitch. Standing on Route 2 at the junction of Interstate 190, which goes to Wickburg thirty-five miles away, I am aware of the rotten things that can happen.

I brace myself against the traffic, especially the big trucks that almost suck me down and under, between the axles, with the *whoosh* of their passing.

Finally a small red car stops and I run to it. A guy is alone in the car. He is sleek and elegant. The smell of aftershave emerges from the car as the window slides down. A briefcase is on the front seat. He smiles, a fake salesman smile, and his hand is between his legs. "Hello there, sweetheart," he says. "Jump in."

"Take off, sicko," I tell him.

Meanness shoots out of his eyes and the window flashes up, almost catching my hand, and the car peels off, spitting up a cloud of dust.

Cars keep passing by and I don't always stick out my

thumb. I see them approaching and try to figure out what kind of person is driving. I skip sports cars, of course, and ignore pick-up trucks. If I see something like dice dangling above the windshield, I also skip that one. Finally, a blue van approaches, dusty, needing a good wash. The handle of what is probably a lawn-mower sticks out of the side window. I stick out my thumb, arrange what I hope is a pleasant expression on my face. The van doesn't stop. I shrug and turn away but something makes me turn back. The van is backing up, approaching me in reverse.

As I open the door and slip in, the driver squints at me, worry lines creasing his forehead. I figure he's in his middle thirties. He is nice looking, neat. He is wearing a blue sports shirt open at the neck. His eyes, too, are blue.

I settle into the seat, shifting my backpack to the floor at my feet, and turn to see him looking doubtful about my presence. I want to ask him what's the matter but I know what's the matter.

"Going to Providence?" I ask. I never tell them my real destination and I know this man with his lawn-mower is not going all the way to Providence.

"Monument," he says. "Is that far enough?" Then: "I never did this before. I mean, this is something I never do, pick up a hitch-hiker."

Especially a young girl.

"I'm glad you did," I tell him. I smile at him. I am aware of my short shorts and move my legs.

He looks at me for a long moment. He is trying not to look at my legs, but he looks anyway. Quickly, then away. As the car begins to move, he asks, "Why are you going to Providence?" Then immediately: "I'm sorry. I don't mean to pry."

I am not lonesome any more. He seems gentle, someone who would be tender. I spread my legs a little more and sigh, my shoulders at attention, knowing what this does to my top.

A breeze drifts through the open window in the rear of the car. Perspiration dampens his forehead. He smiles at me, an uncertain smile.

We are in the country, long fields on either side of the highway, trees shimmering in the heat, bushes heavy at the side of the road. His knuckles are white as he grips the steering wheel. His Adam's apple jiggles as he swallows.

"Would you like to kiss me?" I ask, the words popping out unexpectedly. Although I think it would be nice to be kissed and held by him.

I am surprised to see a grown-up person blush. His hands, trembling, leave the steering wheel for a wild moment and the car swerves. He grabs the wheel again.

He opens his mouth to speak but no words come out.

"You seem very nice," I say. Much nicer than the CD guy. "And the way you look at me, I think you'd like to kiss me. Make out a little."

I know this about him: he has maybe dreamed about something like this—otherwise, why did he stop to pick me up?—and I am his dream come true. I also know that I can handle him: that gentleness about him.

"Why don't you pull over?" I say. "Seems like a lot of places we can stop." The CD guy only gave me CDs and videos. Maybe this man can give me more. I need all the money I can get if I'm going to stay away.

"Why?" he asks desperately, his voice a whisper, his eyes agonizing.

"Because I like you," I say. Then: "And maybe you could help me out a little. Like, say, twenty dollars . . ."

He keeps his eyes on the road. A vein leaps in his temple, seems about to burst. This is the moment when he will decide what to do. I don't move. I don't do anything with my legs or my top. I realize I am holding my breath.

"I never did anything like this before," he says.

"I know, I know." Like he's the young person and I'm the old one.

He pulls into a spot by the side of the road, eases into a place that's hidden from passing cars. The handle of the lawn-mower bumps against the window glass as we stop.

He reaches for me, eyes closed, and I go towards him, letting him have me, and he kisses my cheeks and throat and his hands move over my body. He makes a funny moaning sound when he touches my top and his hand remains there, caressing. I begin to drift with it all, letting him squeeze and caress, and he's not rough at all, his fingers trembling sometimes. I open my mouth to him and he moans again as he kisses me and he is all over me now, and I let him continue because he is tender with his touch. He is breathing fast, too, gasping as he takes his lips away, his heart throbbing against me, and suddenly he shudders like an earthquake throughout his body and I know he is finished. He curls up on the seat beside me, his head turned away.

And he's, like, crying.

I have never seen a man cry before.

I touch his shoulder and he looks at me and his face makes me angry at myself because it's the saddest face in the world and I made him sad.

He looks down and sees my wrists.

"What's that?" he says, sniffling, the way little kids do when the tears stop but the hurt goes on.

"A dog bit me there. A wild bull terrier."

If you are going to lie, you have to be specific, not vague. Words are very important. Like with *bull terrier*. Which sounds authentic even though I haven't the slightest notion what a bull terrier looks like. In the fifth grade, old Mr Stuyvesant told me about lying. He was the handyman at the project and would put me on his lap and tell me lots of good stuff. His touch was always gentle.

"Twenty dollars," I say, holding out my hand, trying to ignore his wet cheeks and trying also to ignore this surge of guilt within me.

He wipes his cheeks with a frayed Kleenex he pulls out of his pocket. He takes out his wallet and removes a twenty-dollar bill and a ten-dollar bill and places them in my hand.

A tip. A ten-dollar tip, for crying out loud.

"I'm sorry," he says. "I . . ."

"I know," I say. "You never did this before." But I say it sincerely and not sarcastically, because I believe him. I almost ask him about his wife and children. I am sure he has a nice wife and maybe three children, two boys and a girl, the oldest one about my age. Maybe that's why he cried afterwards.

He gets prepared to drive away again and puts his wallet in his pocket, but it slips out and wedges in the small space between the front seats. As he pulls out into the highway, I slowly reach out my hand and pick up the wallet, moving my body all around and opening my legs again just in case he looks my way. I slip the wallet into my pocket.

We drive in silence, his eyes fastened on the road ahead,

and I don't say anything, nothing I can say to make him feel better.

He lets me off on the outskirts of Monument.

As I open the door to leave, he touches my shoulder, then draws his hand back quickly. I look at him, and the sorrow is gone from his eyes now and I see in them what I saw before. He wants me to get back in.

I shake my head.

"I'm sorry," he says.

"It's been nice meeting you," I tell him, thinking of his wallet in my pocket.

Sometimes I am a real bitch.

His wallet contains two twenty-dollar bills and three ones. Forty-three dollars. He must have just drawn money from an ATM: the bills are clean and crisp. Combined with my own thirty-three dollars gives me a grand total of, what? seventy-six. Plus change.

From one compartment I remove his driver's licence. His name is Walter R. Clayton. His date of birth is 16–7–58. His height is 5′ 9″. His sex, of course, is M. He lives at 38 Humberton Road, Monument. His picture is not very flattering.

This compartment also holds his Blue Cross/Blue Shield card with his identification number, an ATM card from Wachusett Savings, a tucked-away ten-dollar bill (for emergencies?) folded between two credit cards, VISA and MasterCard.

The other compartment contains two photographs. One picture shows a blonde girl, maybe twelve or thirteen, squinting at the camera as if the sun is hurting her eyes. She's not very pretty. On the back of the photo is her name, Karen, no date. She is in the other picture, too, posing with a boy who is two or three years younger. He's identified on the back as Kevin. The girl is nice-looking in this picture, blonde hair shining and a big smile on her face. Kevin looks solemn, as if he'd rather be out somewhere playing baseball.

I am sitting on a log by the side of the highway, protected from view by some bushes. I hear the traffic going by as I study the stuff in the wallet. I put it all back and sit still, not looking at anything in particular.

This is not the first time I have stolen something, but it's the first time I have stolen from a person, someone with a name. Walter R. Clayton, a man with a family. I wonder why he didn't carry a picture of his wife. Maybe he is divorced. Maybe she is dead. Or maybe she held the camera, which is why she isn't in the picture—I'd like to think that. Anyway, stealing from Walter Clayton is different from stealing from an impersonal place like a store. Stealing from a store doesn't make you feel too bad afterwards, not like how I feel knowing that Walter Clayton has lost not only his money but his credit cards and driver's licence, and all the trouble he faces getting new ones. Plus explaining to his wife how he lost his wallet and having to lie about it. Or maybe this will teach him a lesson, not to pick up young girls in his car and pay them to let him touch and hold them. I remember how he cried afterwards. I decide that when I get to Wickburg I will get an envelope and stamps and mail his credit cards and his licence and the pictures, too, back to him.

I finally reached Wickburg by late afternoon. I walked most of the way, trudging along 190, not sticking out my thumb, tired of judging what kind of car or driver was approaching. I was not in the mood for more adventures on the road.

Finally, a car pulled up. I looked at it suspiciously but saw the handicapped licence plate. A woman with grey hair opened the passenger door and asked me if I wanted a lift. That's what she called it: a lift. I glanced into the car and saw the driver, who also had grey hair. There were all kinds of gadgets attached to the steering wheel. Their voices were kindly. They both had mild grey eyes. The driver looked cheerful, despite all the gadgets on the steering wheel. I couldn't see his legs. "You look bushed," the woman said. "Like you need to sit back and rest awhile . . ." That's what she said: *bushed*.

I guess she meant I looked tired. Which I was, tired and hot, my underarms moist.

The man turned on the radio as we pulled away. Country music filled the air, a sad song about somebody's lost love dancing in a bar. I tried to blot out the music and call to mind the bang and boom of Throb and those words of his:

Eat my heart
Chew it hard
Swallow my soul, too.

I fell asleep like falling into a deep well with quiet waters lapping at my bones as they melted.

They let me off at Main and Madison in downtown Wickburg, three blocks from the ConCentre. I felt bad because I had slept most of the way and barely talked to them.

"Thank you," I called after them as they drove away.

I don't think they heard me. And I instantly forgot all about them as I looked up at a billboard on the roof of a bank building showing a huge picture of Throb in his crazy costume and that black hole in his mouth.

I am standing in the alley between the Marriott and the Brice office building, and I'm looking at the doorway in the wall of the Marriott that does not look like a doorway. It's a secret doorway used by the superstars to escape from the crowds at the front and rear entrances of the hotel so that they can make their way unobserved to the ConCentre a block away.

The area around the Marriott is jammed with fans along with police and security people, and I find a quiet spot near the Dumpster in the alley. I have taken a long skirt from my backpack and am wearing it over my shorts. A breeze stirs the debris in the alley but brings no relief from the evening heat. In fact, the breeze stirs up the smell of garbage from the Dumpster and something decaying inside. I fix my eyes on the secret doorway.

Suddenly, out he comes: Throb. Four or five people, like bodyguards, emerging with him. He's dressed in his crazy costume, Sunkist hair and baggy pants, no shirt, plus something new: ear-rings dangling from his nipples. He yawns, actually yawns, and I see the hole in his mouth and this sends me into action.

I lunge across the alley, covering the few feet between us like a bowling ball, knocking aside the bodyguards, and I am directly in front of him. His eyes widen in disbelief and his eyes are mean, green, and red streaked. They eat into me, those eyes.

His bodyguards are still recovering from my surprise attack, not quite sure what to do, but I know what I must do. I must kiss him. More than that, I must put my tongue in that hole in his mouth and end this fixation. I reach out and cup his face in my hands and plant this monstrous kiss on his mouth, my lips devouring his mouth, my tongue slipping between his lips, tasting whiskey and something else on his breath. My tongue is between his teeth in that hole and now the bodyguards are pulling at me and yelling, but Throb is transfixed as if hypnotized. I tear myself away from the groping hands and run, half-tripping over my skirt, my backpack bouncing, spitting out the taste of him as I go. I streak into the crowd at the mouth of the alley as the crowd surges forward, spotting Throb finally. I am still spitting out the taste of him as I lose myself in the jostling, bustling crowd, knowing that my fixation is over and I can go on with life, whatever that life will be.

I have to think about my options now, what I will do tonight and where to stay, and I slip into the Wickburg Diner, all stainless steel and glass, which looks like a railroad dining car, a place I used to go when my mother and I lived in Wickburg.

I order coffee and a hamburger and sit in the booth, the plastic covering cool on my back and air-conditioning a nice cold stream on my shoulders.

A television set hangs from the ceiling, and I try to blot out the voices and pictures as I wait for the food. I am not really hungry but my stomach is empty and I feel the need to nourish myself. The smell of fried food sizzles in the air, always a lonesome smell to me, not homey like pies being baked or a roast in the oven, which my mother always cooks when we first settle into a new place but never later.

Two girls sit in the next booth, giggling and laughing and then whispering to each other. They are not really girls, and I know who they are. Not their names, of course, but *what* they are. They're like the girls I have seen cruising the streets, carrying cheap plastic handbags, something sad about them despite the laughing and the make-up. The one facing me has deep, dark eyes, and the other is a blonde.

I look up at the television set but see only images and hear only sound. I blot out the rest. I am good at this, blotting out things I don't want to acknowledge, like lying awake in my room at night while Gary and my mother are in the next room and I remove my thoughts, my ears from what's going on.

But the television intrudes now, a face flashing on the screen that brings me back to here and now. I know that face. An off-screen voice reaches my ears:

". . . being set free Friday. The state cannot hold him any longer and thus a murderer will be loose among us . . ."

Now a scene outside a prison, a crowd, and a guy emerging from a police cruiser, being rushed into a court-house. The guy turns and faces the camera. I see his eyes, eyes that I remember, and the way his lips curl into a smile but a smile like no other smile in the world. The announcer's voice continues:

". . . shown arriving at the Polk County Court-house for his final appearance . . . has remained silent throughout his incarceration after having been found guilty by the juvenile court judge of two counts of murder . . ."

"I wouldn't mind being incarcerated with him," the blonde in the next booth says.

"But he's a murderer," the dark-eyed girl says.

"What a way to die," the first one responds.

Now his face is on the screen again, close up, those eyes staring at the camera as if staring at nobody and nothing and then breaking into a sudden, startling smile. That smile does it, and I remember that smile from a faraway day when my mother and I were living here in Wickburg and how those eyes looked at me and I remember, too, the sound of his voice: "Happy birthday." That's what he said to me, the words echoing now in my mind. I hear a small moan and know immediately that it is me who has moaned because I am fixated again, on him, so soon, too soon, after Throb.

But nothing I can do about it.

The TV voice again:

"Eric Poole has remained silent about his future plans but rumours indicate he will be staying with his aunt in Wickburg, Massachusetts, and already neighbours are protesting about a murderer in their neighbourhood . . ."

Now a shot of a street, regular houses, cottages, with picket fences and trees along the sidewalk and people gathering, some of them with signs, although the camera moves too fast to catch what the signs say.

I blot it all out, close my eyes and my ears to the voices and images on the television.

But his face emerges from the darkness behind my eyes.

I am fixated again, all right, and I can't help myself and know that I must find Eric Poole and kiss him, press my lips against his lips, my tongue against his tongue, the only way I will end this new fixation of mine.

Eric Poole began with cats. Or, to be more exact, kittens. Liked to hold them, and stroke them, feel the brittle bones beneath the fur. Fragile bones, as if they'd snap and break if you pressed too hard, caressed too hard. Which he did, of course, impossible to resist. Later, he didn't just caress them but found that it was easier to fold them into his arms and place his hands over their faces and feel them go beautifully limp. He liked this way best, because it was so tender. Inevitably, kittens grew into cats and it wasn't the same. Cats were not so trusting, had resistance. Needed more drastic measures, which he hated. Hated drastic measures. Hated violence but sometimes couldn't help it. Had to follow the demands and the dictates of the situation. As a result, he used more strenuous methods. And got used to it. Enjoyed it, in fact. Just cleaning up the neighbourhood, he told himself. Crooned the words, as he did his job. The real problem was disposal. Cleaning up the neighbourhood of the feline population, he pondered the problem. And found the obvious solution: burial. Which meant getting a shovel. And digging. And sweating. He didn't like to sweat. Didn't like his body's aromas wafting on the air for other people to absorb. Yet the exercise was good. He didn't get enough exercise. That's what his mother always said. His mother wanted him to be more active. Do things. Help around the house. Go places, if only to the mall. She wanted to get rid of him, of course, so she could have Harvey to herself.

So he went to the mall. Where he graduated. From cats and kittens and Aunt Phoebe's canary. The canary was the only representative of the feathered-friend population to receive his attention. Couldn't resist doing it even though it invited suspicion for the first time.

"How did Rudy get out of the cage?" Aunt Phoebe asked, mystified.

Rudy, a ridiculous name for a canary.

"Maybe the latch got loose," he suggested, face all innocent. He had an innocent face. His face was also beautiful. Innocence and beauty, always confirmed when he looked into a mirror, which he often did.

"Rudy was a clever bird," he told Aunt Phoebe. "Maybe he opened the latch with his beak and flew around and crashed into the wall." Amused as he told her this, seeing her expression of mixed emotions: sad and mystified. Really sad, as she held little Rudy cupped in her hands. Poor thing, crushed like that, so easy, a quick snapping sound and it was over and done with. Tears in Aunt Phoebe's eyes. Over a bird, of all things.

Dispatching Rudy was the highlight of his vacation that year with Aunt Phoebe in Wickburg.

Back home, visiting the mall, there was a pet store with small animals of all kinds, locked up nice and safe in cages. He regarded them without curiosity. He was tired of the animal population, anyway.

What did that leave?

He watched the people shopping, carrying bundles. Or just hanging out. Old people sitting on the yellow plastic benches, talking mildly to each other. Other people rushing past the stores, in a hurry, going somewhere. Teenagers in their oversized clothes, shirts hanging out, pants bunched stupidly at the ankles, baseball caps turned around. The girls looked really terrible, garish colours, crazy ear-rings, too much lipstick, hair going every which way, some with ear-rings in their nostrils and insolence on their faces, in their eyes.

He always dressed neatly. Clean clothes. Nikes all laced up, jacket without a spot. But not too neat. Did not want to draw attention to himself, did not want to invite inspection. Especially by those teenage girls with the insolent eyes. Or the watery eyes of old people.

Which would it be? A girl or someone old?

The questions surprised him, because he had not contemplated doing anything, *anyone* in particular, preferred to let chance take over, drift with whatever happened. Like with the kittens, cats, and even Rudy. Never plan in advance, go with the flow, follow his instincts. But knew it had to be different now. Suspicions. Investigations. That meant planning, scheming, which made it all kind of exciting.

Excitement was a new experience for him.

He seldom, if ever, felt excited about anything. But did not feel bored, either. Lived in a place between both, with the expectation of something big happening or about to happen. Went through the motions at school, made good grades, faithful with homework, amassed facts and figures and spewed them out as required, made honours without really trying, the computer doing most of the work. Made the teachers happy, his mother, even Harvey, who managed a stingy smile once in a while. But the hell with Harvey. He would put up with Harvey and his mother until situations changed. Meanwhile, he kept out of Harvey's way and spent more time at the mall. Banners proclaimed that it was the Second Biggest Mall in New England although he didn't think the second biggest of anything was much to brag about, but the mall was a more interesting place than home. For instance, he was amazed at the change of seasons at the mall. The mall, actually, was without weather, without sun or moon or stars or wind or rain or snow. Yet the seasons were in constant rotation, Christmas and Valentine's Day and Mother's Day, the colours and displays and decorations following the calendar. Saint Patrick's Day, leprechauns and shamrocks, and Easter with bunnies and coloured eggs everywhere. At the moment, however, the mall was between holidays, a pause after Mother's Day and before the Fourth of July.

Waiting for a situation to develop, he began to ration his visits there. Did not linger in one particular section. Made small purchases, always carried a package of some sort. Did not always make a purchase but chose from a collection of plastic bags at home from Walden Books or Hallmark or Strawberries, which he filled with any old thing so that he looked like a paying customer. He began to disguise himself in small ways. Dressed more like other teenagers, although he disliked wearing baggy clothes that didn't fit well. He visited a thrift shop downtown and bought second-hand stuff. Hated wearing clothing other people had worn but made himself do it. Combed his hair differently, sometimes with bangs, other times flat and sleek like an old-time movie star. Wore his arm in a sling occasionally. Other times pretended to limp.

The mall was two and a half miles from his house, and sometimes Harvey drove him there, glad to be rid of him for a while. Other times he took the bus, although he hated riding the bus, confined in close quarters with other people, who coughed and sweated, inhaled and exhaled, but he sacrificed his personal wants and desires to the cause.

What cause?

He didn't know. But felt that he was involved in some great future event. And had to be ready when it happened.

Then it happened.

He spotted the girl late one afternoon. She was tall, with dark hair flowing to her shoulders, slender, cool, wearing a white blouse and brown slacks.

She carried herself aloof as if she were balancing a book on her head.

He began to follow her, limping a bit. He had chosen this day to affect a limp, dragging his right foot as he walked. He was careful to keep her in view, not too distant from her, not too near. The mall was crowded. Thursday was pay-day at the local mills and factories, and workers streamed in to cash their cheques at one of the bank branches, eat at McDonald's or Friendly's, and go on small shopping sprees.

The girl headed towards Exit E, perfect for his purposes, the distant end of the mall, woods less than the length of a football field away from the bus stop. He watched as the doors opened automatically for her departure. Careful to keep limping, he managed to quicken his pace, all senses keen and alert, colours everywhere bright and vivid, his step unable to keep pace with his hastening heart.

"My problem, Eric, is your lack of remorse."

"But that's my problem, not yours."

"And your insolence."

"I don't mean to be insolent. I'm truthful. I tell the truth and the truth sometimes hurts. For instance, you have bad breath, Lieutenant. I can smell it from here. It must offend a lot of people. That's the truth. But how many people have told you that? Instead, they either lie or try to avoid your company."

Actually, Eric did not know whether or not the lieutenant had bad breath. But enjoyed baiting him, watching for his reaction. Was there a faint blush now emerging on his cheeks?

"Your smooth talk. That's a problem, too," the lieutenant said, continuing the verbal assault for which Eric admired him, not a whole lot but somewhat.

"Look, Lieutenant, we know what the problem is, right? Not my lack of remorse or my smooth talk. The problem is that I'm turning eighteen in three days. The state says that I can't be held any longer. That's the problem, isn't it?"

The lieutenant said nothing. He was an old man, crevices in his face, sorrowful blue eyes, wispy grey hair. He smoked endless cigarettes, the ashes falling indiscriminately on his shirt or tie. His jacket never matched his trousers. He had been one of the arresting officers three years ago and had slipped the handcuffs on Eric's wrists. Then began visiting Eric after he started serving his sentence. He had been coming to the facility four times a year, at each change of season, for the three years Eric had been incarcerated.

"Why do you keep coming here?" Eric asked at the end of the first year.

"Why do you keep seeing me?" the lieutenant countered. Like a teacher making the student answer.

"Isn't it about time for you to retire? You look old and tired," Eric said, without sympathy in his voice. The old man looked sad, too, but Eric remained silent about that.

"What would I do if I retired? I don't have any hobbies,

and no family. They give me easy cases. Wait a minute—you're my hobby, Eric. Finding out what makes you tick. Like you're the broken watch and I'm the repair man."

"Who says the watch is broken?" Eric asked, annoyed, but the old cop hadn't answered, merely lit another cigarette.

Which was exactly what he was doing now, probably the final cigarette on this, his final visit.

"You're a psychopath, Eric." The smoke came out of the lieutenant's mouth as if his words were stoked by an inner fire. "A monster."

Eric recoiled, as if the old cop had struck him in the face. Monster?

"Chances are you'll kill again. You know it and I know it."

Or was the old cop merely trying to taunt him? Trying to make him lose his cool? *Don't let him do that. Monster* was only a word, anyway. And those were the only weapons the lieutenant had: words.

"You're taking a lot for granted, Lieutenant," Eric said, the sound of his voice reassuring, establishing his control of the conversation once more. "You're making wild accusations. I wasn't even convicted by a jury. A judge heard my case. He didn't think I was a monster. He was very sympathetic. So were a lot of other people."

"Other people? Did you take a close look at them? Who they were, what they were? You killed your mother and father, Eric. In cold blood." Not sounding tired any more.

Eric did not smile but his eyes gleamed. The lieutenant did not know about the others. Nobody knew about them.

"Harvey was not my father," Eric said, leaving behind the thoughts of others. "He was my stepfather. I had just cause, Lieutenant. All that pain . . ."

"What do you know about pain?" the old cop snorted.

"You don't even allow me my pain, do you, Lieutenant?"

He had stolen three cigarettes from Harvey's pack of Marlboros. Went to the shed in the backyard, his hideaway, the shed tucked under overgrown maples, branches almost hiding the doorway. A combination lock prevented entry by anyone but himself. His retreat from the world. When he was tired of his mother and Harvey, the mall, school, everything, he went to the shed and just sat there. On the old revolving office chair. "What do you do in there, anyway?" Harvey often asked, suspicious, always suspicious of everybody and everything. "Nothing," Eric answered. Most times he didn't bother answering Harvey, which he knew made Harvey furious. He only answered him when he could score points. Actually, *nothing* was an honest answer. Because he did nothing in the shed but simply sit there and think. Or didn't even think. Let himself become blank. Like sleeping while awake.

But now he did not simply sit there and think. Instead, he set about doing what he had to do. Opened the only window a bit, to let the smoke out. Lucky the window faced the woods, away from the house. Lit the first cigarette, did not inhale, grimaced at the invasion of smoke in his face and eyes, the taste of it in his mouth. Looked curiously at the glowing tip. Placing the cigarette on the cover of a mayonnaise jar serving as an ashtray, he rolled up his left sleeve. Smooth and pale skin. Tapped the ash from the cigarette, studied the burning end for a moment, then braced himself and pressed the burning tip against his flesh.

Taken by surprise by the sheer ferocity of the pain, he

uttered a single syllable of agony: *Ahhhh*. Then shut his mouth, clamping it tight, pressing his lips together. The burning tip fell off the cigarette and dropped to the floor. He stepped on it, still absorbing the pain in his arm, reluctant to look at it. With trembling fingers, he lit another cigarette, eyes slitted against the enveloping smoke, and through moist eyes watched himself place the burning end of the new cigarette against his flesh, an inch or two from the first spot. Grimacing, he gasped, emitted a muffled scream through his lips. Seeing the tip end still glowing red, he pressed it against another spot on his arm, learning that pain reaches a certain point and does not get worse but remains in all its intensity and you can survive it. But, Christ, how it hurt . . . causing strange things to happen to his body, a wave of nausea sweeping his stomach, his knees turning weak and watery, and his head swimming with sudden dizziness that made the room whirl sickeningly until everything settled into place again. He held his arm stiffly in front of him, making himself look at those three cruel scorched places, could smell his burning flesh — no, not flesh, but the small hairs on his arm, singed and blackened now.

He suddenly leaped from a flash of more pain, this time unexpected. He'd been holding the second cigarette between the first two fingers of his right hand, and the cigarette had burned down to his flesh. He dropped it, stepped on it. Then he extended his arm again and smiled grimly as he inspected the three burned places.

He had also planned to use the hammer today but decided the burning was enough this time. He would put the hammer to work tomorrow. Looking at the vice fastened to the edge of the work-table, he wondered how he could use it to facilitate breaking his arm. Might be better than using just the hammer.

"You're a menace to society, Eric. Because you are incapable of feeling. Have you ever really felt anything? Sad? Or sorry? Sorry for what you did to your mother, your stepfather? Sorry for anything at all? In fact, have you ever even felt happy? That's what makes you a psychopath, Eric. You are incapable of connecting with other people. Emotion, that's what connects us all. Without emotion, without feeling, we're nothing. We're animals. Zeros, ciphers."

"I read somewhere that swans mate for life, Lieutenant. Must be some kind of feeling involved there, some kind of emotion. Maybe animals know more about emotions than we give them credit for . . ."

Eric liked these verbal games with the old lieutenant. He knew he could talk circles around him. His smooth talk was actually for the lieutenant's benefit. Ordinarily he didn't have much to say to anyone, especially in this place. Talking to the old man, baiting him now and then, broke the monotony of the facility.

"Stop playing games, Eric. You know very well what I mean about lack of feeling . . ."

Ah, but he had felt bad about the girl at the mall. Holding her limp body in his arms afterwards, cradling her gently, he had seen that her make-up was too heavy. His fingers stroked her long black hair. He opened her mouth and counted five fillings. But he had no time for further inspection because footfalls reached his ears, along with the crackling of bushes being pushed aside. Someone was nearby and coming closer. He crouched down, the girl beneath him, stilling himself, listening to the crunch of footsteps passing by and then receding, growing faint. Then silence again, except for the distant sounds of cars on the highway. He sighed with relief and vowed to be more careful in the future.

It had been so easy to lure the girl away from the mall. First of all, he had dropped the limping act once he followed her out the door. Outside, in the chilled twilight air, he had spotted her waiting at the bus stop. No one else was in sight. He approached her and turned on The Charm. Ever since he was a little kid, The Charm had worked wonders. That smile, along with his blond hair and blue eyes. When he smiled, something happened to his eyes. His eyes seemed to smile, too, sort of glowed. Irresistible. He had watched The Charm happen when he studied himself in a mirror. *What a sweet little boy*, he heard people say when he was just a child. And later: *a great-looking boy you've got there, Mrs Poole.* Eric was tall and slender. At fifteen, he was almost six feet tall. Girls flirted with him at school but he didn't respond. Boys stayed away from him and he didn't mind. He preferred to be alone. He found himself reflected in other people's attitudes. Basked in their admiration. Or seemed to. Yet not everyone was affected by The Charm. Some people were indifferent. Some people he could not win over. A teacher now and then. People who regarded him with indifference or simply turned away, unimpressed, even suspicious. Maybe a store clerk or a bus driver. Specifically, Ginger Rowell, whom he'd asked to the Spring Dance in the eighth grade. He'd had no inclination to go to the Spring Dance, but his mother kept hounding him about it. "Everybody wants to go to the Spring Dance," she insisted. "Everybody normal, that is." Which stung him. Normal? So he asked Ginger Rowell. Who was nothing special although pretty and energetic and a cheer-leader. She looked at him with cool appraising eyes and said: "No thanks." Humiliating him, leaving him staring in disbelief as she walked away. So he had learned early on that there were people who did not respond properly to The Charm and he stayed away from them, ignored them, set them apart from his life, as if they did not exist.

His mother was a puzzle to him. She usually looked at him with the tender eyes of love. Always kissed him goodnight, a kiss that left a moist spot on his cheek. He dimly remembered good times when he was a small kid and they'd cuddle in bed. But he didn't like to think of those times after Harvey came along. Once in a while he caught his mother studying him, eyes narrowed, as if she were regarding a stranger.

He was always a dutiful son. He kept his room clean. He made no fuss when she sent him on errands, even when it was inconvenient. He never played his CDs too loud. He was not insolent, never answered back when she said stupid things. She had a habit of saying everything twice: *It's cold out. It's cold out.* Or *Did you have a good day at school today? Did you have a good day at school today?* He put up with that, sometimes joked with her about it, didn't let it get on his nerves. But it got on Harvey's nerves. A lot of things got on Harvey's nerves. Eric was the major thing. They hated each other at first sight. Amend that: Eric did not hate him. Harvey was not worth hating. He was such an ugly specimen of humanity. *What does she see in him?* That was the question to which Eric never found an answer.

He thought of his mother and Ginger Rowell as he held the limp body of the girl in his arms. He pictured Ginger Rowell lying close to him like this, but he immediately rejected the image. Ginger was small and blonde; this girl was tall and dark. Anyway, Ginger had seen something in his eyes that Eric knew existed and he could not fault her for that, despite the humiliation. His mother had caused the humiliation when she had forced him to ask Ginger to the dance. For the first time, the glimmer of what he would some day do to his mother and Harvey, like the winking of a distant star, appeared in his consciousness.

As Eric lay beside the girl, ignoring the cheap perfume in his nostrils, he sighed with contentment. Finally, he laid her gently to rest in the bushes, carefully brushing back a strand of hair from her face. That black hair. Her left arm fell loose, pale and fragile. For some reason, he trailed his mouth along her flesh, so warm and moist against his lips. Bliss filled him. He had never known such tenderness before, his body trembling with it. He knew that he must find it again.

"Your plans, Eric. Do you want to discuss them?"

The old lieutenant's voice had gentled. "Where you're going, what you're going to do. You've had no visitors here. Haven't had any mail for a long time . . ."

Eric had been deluged with mail when he first arrived at the facility. Letters from kids who thought he was some kind of hero. Or a martyr or a victim. Most of the mail from teenage girls, who also sent pictures of themselves, cheap photos made in machines at the malls for a dollar. Some letters had lipstick kisses on them, promises and pledges. *I will wait for you for ever.* Letters and postcards from skinheads, neo-Nazis, grotesques, and freaks that Eric tossed aside without answering.

After a while, he stopped reading the letters and postcards. Had never answered them in the first place and had ignored requests for his autograph. He distributed to the other inmates the gifts he received, home-made cakes and cookies, elaborate hand-made greeting cards, neckties, a few boxes of condoms. The inmates clamoured for his letters, so that they could write to the girls who'd sent them, but Eric refused to hand them over. Why inflict these sorry specimens, these losers, on poor, unsuspecting girls? Which did not earn Eric any points from the other prisoners, despite the candy and cake he turned over to them. Eric viewed his fellow prisoners with indifference. He didn't want to make friends. Or enemies. He simply wanted to be left alone, to avoid stupid conversations, to serve his time without trouble or fuss of any kind. Which was easy. As the only murderer in the facility, he lived, for the most part, separately from the other prisoners. He shared classrooms, duties and meals with them. But his room was in a different wing of the facility. He took his recreational activities alone, strolling the grounds by himself when other prisoners were inside. He was not allowed to participate in team sports, watched baseball games from his second-floor window. He enjoyed his solitude. Most of the other prisoners were stupid, caught for petty crimes that anyone with intelligence wouldn't commit in the first place and certainly wouldn't be dumb enough to be caught doing.

His case had drawn national attention when authorities attempted to try him as an adult for the murders of his mother and stepfather. It was two months after his fifteenth birthday. He had remained silent during the frenzy of publicity, granted no interviews, made no statements. When he allowed himself to be photographed, he was careful to smile for the camera, not the smile of The Charmer but a sad, wistful smile that he calculated would soften his image. The clincher came when he faced the cameras outside police headquarters after his arrest. Slowly and deliberately, he pushed up his sleeves and revealed the scars from the cigarette burns on his arm, the bruise that remained from his broken arm. The wounds were silent and compelling evidence of the abuse he had received from his stepfather, abuse that, he told his interrogators, his mother had not only condoned but encouraged.

Support for him came immediately, not only from the freaks who sent him letters and gifts, but from college professors, newspapers as far away as Boston. They had played right into his hands. None of those who supported him cared to look deeply into his case, letting a few scars on his arm and a sad smile convince them that he had been done wrong. *Kill Your Parents and Become the Victim.* What a wonderful country, he thought.

He was not exonerated, of course, simply because he had confessed to the murders. But the scars and the millions of words from professors and columnists and editorial writers caused the authorities to try him as a juvenile instead of an adult. Which meant that he would be placed in the jurisdiction of the state Department of Youth Services, serving his sentence in a youth facility instead of a state prison. He would be set free, without restrictions, at the age of eighteen, three days from now. And here was the old lieutenant swallowing his anger, asking him his plans.

He had not talked to anyone, counsellors or advisors, about what he would do, where he would go when the facility's doors closed behind him on Friday. He hadn't talked about his plans simply because he did not have to. His freedom was complete and unconditional. He would not be on parole or probation. His records would be sealed. He would not have to report to anybody or account for his future actions. He *did* have plans, of course. Long-range plans. Which were nobody's business. But his immediate plans were different. Telling the old lieutenant about them would serve a useful purpose.

"I'm going to live with my Aunt Phoebe, in Wickburg, up in Massachusetts, until I decide what to do about the future."

The lieutenant looked sceptical.

"She's never visited you here. Does she know about your plans?"

"Aunt Phoebe doesn't like to travel and I didn't want her to see me in this place. We've been writing to each other. I was allowed to make a long-distance phone call to her last week. She said she would be glad to take me in. She's my mother's sister."

"Any job prospects? You finished high school here, earned your GED. You did very well in the machine shop . . ."

Eric hated the machine shop. Had caught on fast to the demands and intricacies of tool and die making but did not plan to earn his living that way.

"College maybe. I just want to pace myself for a while."

"The news media will be a factor, Eric. You're going to be hounded. They'll be waiting for you when you step out of here. They'll follow you to your Aunt Phoebe's place. They'll be on the watch night and day. You're the last of a breed, Eric. Things are changing on the outside. New laws are being passed. Stiffer penalties for juveniles who commit serious crimes. More of them are now being tried as adults — "

"That has nothing to do with me, Lieutenant," Eric interrupted. He knew that it was time for him to make his pitch, to resurrect The Charm, and convince the old cop that he had changed.

"I want to make something of myself," he said, allowing

the wistful smile to appear. "They say your body changes every few years. Well, I came here just turned fifteen and I'm leaving at eighteen and I'm a different person. The kid who killed his mother and stepfather was somebody else. I want to make a new start . . ."

Too much charm? Or too little? Had he sounded sincere?

The lieutenant gazed at him steadily for a moment without expression. He stubbed out his cigarette in a glass ashtray, tried to rub the ashes off his tie but they remained. Probably from an earlier cigarette. He reached for his beat-up old briefcase, opened it, and extracted a big yellow pad with ruled lines. He scrutinized a series of scribbles on the pad, frowning. Then began to read in a flat, toneless voice:

"Laura Andersun. Fifteen years of age. Body found in bushes near Greenhill Mall. Strangled. Sexually assaulted, probably after death occurred."

Then looked up, straight into Eric's eyes.

So much for The Charm, Eric thought. So much for sincerity.

"That's old stuff, Lieutenant. I was never charged with Laura Andersun's death. Questioned, yes, because it happened the same year my mother and stepfather died. A big coincidence. But no charges were brought. There was no motive."

"Psychopaths don't need a motive," the old cop said.

"Witnesses reported the girl was being followed by a cripple," Eric said. "Someone with a bad leg, someone who limped."

"A bad leg, a limp can be easily faked," the lieutenant said, voice still flat, deadly.

His eyes returned to the pad.

"Betty Ann Tersa," he recited. "Sixteen. Disappeared six weeks after Laura Andersun's death. A month before your mother and Harvey died. Still missing. But believed dead."

Eric was genuinely surprised and kept his face blank, stilling himself. No one had ever questioned him about Betty Ann Tersa. Her name had never been mentioned to him. He kept his eyes away from the pad, did not want the lieutenant to see him searching for another name, a third girl, that no one knew about.

"Betty Ann Tersa," Eric mused, allowing the name to form on his lips and bringing back that moment of tenderness behind the dump, her black fragrant hair in his mouth. "Her name is vaguely familiar," he said. Her name had appeared in the newspapers at the time, and denying that knowledge would only make the lieutenant more suspicious. "Didn't she live someplace out on the West Coast?"

"Right," the old cop said brightly, as if Eric had answered the right question and won a prize. "But she had relatives here in New England. An uncle and aunt she sometimes visited."

"I didn't know that," Eric said.

"You know it now," the lieutenant said. "Four deaths, Eric. Your mother, your stepfather, Laura Andersun, Betty Ann Tersa. All within months of each other. Extraordinary, wouldn't you say?"

And a fifth that nobody knew about, which made it really *extraordinary,* Eric thought, saying instead: "But you said Betty Ann Tersa's body was never found. Maybe she ran away."

"Oh, she's dead, all right," the old cop said. "Isn't she, Eric?"

Eric shook his head.

"Why are you doing this, Lieutenant? You're about ready to retire, aren't you? You should be enjoying life. How many years do you have left? You should think about things like that."

"Is that a threat, Eric?"

"Of course not, Lieutenant." Trying The Charm again. "I would never threaten you. All I want to do is get out of this place and lead a normal life."

The old cop sighed, his frail shoulders lifting and falling. He turned away and replaced the yellow pad in his briefcase. He stood up, leaning against the table, his old man's stomach bulging slightly against it.

"Guess we won't see each other any more, will we, Lieutenant?" Eric said. "I'm going to miss our meetings." Surprised at the truth of the statement.

The lieutenant's eyes flashed, the weariness and the sadness suddenly gone, replaced by—what? The sly look of success. But what kind of success? "I'll be outside waving goodbye the day you're free," he said. But his eyes and tone of voice were telling Eric that he never expected that day to come.

That was the second surprise the old cop had pulled today—first, the names on the yellow pad and now that flash of triumph.

"Friday," Eric said, and repeated the word for emphasis. "Friday. Wave to me Friday when I leave this place . . ."

The lieutenant did not answer. His silence was ominous. He gathered his briefcase in both arms and pressed it against his chest as if to guard his old bones. He shuffled to the doorway and paused there, looking back, the spark gone from his eyes, the momentary triumph having passed. He looked exactly like what he was. A sad and tired old man who had gone fallen in defeat at the hands of Eric Poole.

Eric dismissed the lieutenant from his mind the moment the door closed. Back in his room, he checked the calendar on the wall and smiled at the red circle around Friday. Glancing at his bed, he saw his book on martial arts lying on the grey spread. The book had been on the window-sill this morning when he left the room. Opening the book, he riffled through the pages, and found a note tucked between pages 72 and 73. The note, in crude handwriting deliberately disguised, said:

A favour for a favour. Watch your step. Don't be provoked or you might not get out Friday. Or at all.

The note was unsigned, but Eric knew who had written it.

He also had learned the secret of that flash of triumph in the old cop's eyes.

Police Lieutenant Jake Proctor's bad dream began again after Eric Poole came into his life. The dream always started with children crying in the distance, out of sight, their cries growing louder and nearer until they came into view. Little girls in white dresses. Running, running, fleeing some terrible object of dread, their eyes blank like unfinished drawings, their screams so fierce that he'd finally vault into wakefulness. As he did now, heart pounding, thin arms and legs trembling.

The old cop sat up in bed, trying to blink away the dream. He lit a cigarette with shaking fingers. He thought he had left the dream behind in Oregon a long time ago. But hadn't, of course.

He crept out of bed, old bones protesting, the cries of the children finally diminishing as he stalked to the kitchen section of the apartment. Dawn, a grey phantom, lurked outside the window. As he drew water into a kettle and placed it on the stove, his thoughts went inevitably to Eric Poole. And Friday. And the plan.

Lewis had been against the plan, of course. He was the state's deputy commissioner of youth services and went by the book, did not like to improvise. Black and white, that was Lewis, never admitting greys. Respected facts, not instincts.

Jake's boss, Chief Harding, didn't mind bending the rules. Which was why Harding had ascended to the top post in the department. Knowing what had happened out in Oregon, he allowed Jake Proctor latitude. "But for Christ's sake be careful. And take care of yourself. You're no longer a kid . . ."

Jake Proctor had been a cop for twenty-six years out in Oregon and the next twenty here in New England. He'd worked all the beats, been praised and promoted regularly and was finally named a detective lieutenant, an office where his instincts and dogged working habits brought him success but never satisfaction. His one devastating failure back in Oregon had tarnished all the triumphs of his career.

That failure focused on an image he could not erase from his mind: the riverbank on the city's outskirts as he watched them bring another child's body up from the swirling waters. Looking at the limp form in the arms of a rescue worker, he was stunned to realize that he had seen her before. She had made her First Communion the Sunday before at St Anthony's Church, where he had been a parishioner all his life. He did not know her name or anything about her but had been struck by her sweet innocence as she came down the aisle in her white dress, hands clasped against her chest, eyes lowered. For the first time he felt the absence of a child in his life and wondered whether he had made a mistake in avoiding marriage or even a close relationship. The child passed by his pew, close enough for him to touch her shoulder.

She had been the third of what proved eventually to be five murders by a serial killer. Five children under the age of ten, snatched and strangled on the first Monday of the month, each murder exactly three months apart. The killer stalked the children like a ghost, leaving no clues behind.

After the fifth murder, the killings stopped. That dreaded first Monday came and went without incident. No child's body turned up. No stunned and weeping parents. Jake Proctor and his crew of detectives congratulated themselves, as if somehow they had actually solved the case, laughing out of a strange nervous relief. That night Jake Proctor dreamed of the crying children for the first time. Afterwards he lay in bed for long minutes, thinking of the child walking down the aisle, those fragile fingers clasped together. He was suddenly glad that he had never married, never had children, and had thus eliminated the pain of impending loss. Why, then, this sudden ache that he finally recognized as loneliness?

Drinking his tea, he glanced out the window at the bleak buildings stark in emerging daylight. This old city in New England resembled the city he had fled in Oregon, needing to make a new start, as far from the scene of his failure as possible, from one coast to another. He immersed himself in the routine of police work. He didn't mind the long hours, working overtime without putting in for extra pay, to relieve young cops with growing families. He spent his spare time chasing down evidence in old, unsolved cases. Work, he found, could be benevolent, filling the hours, the days, the weeks. Until you found that the years had passed by almost unnoticed. The failure in Oregon grew dim and distant in his memory, and the dream did not disturb his sleep any more. Until Eric Poole arrived in his life.

A dim recollection had stirred within him as he sat in the shadows of the interrogation room watching his colleagues question Eric Poole. He instantly recalled someone he had dismissed from his mind twenty years before, the only suspect in the Oregon murders. His name came to Jake Proctor out of the mists of memory—Derek Larrington. He'd been found in the vicinity of the river in which the body of that First Communion child, and later a red-haired child named Susan Crone, had been thrown. Derek Larrington had been polite, eager to help, answering questions without hesitation. He had recently graduated with honours from a local high school and was working that summer as a waiter to put away money towards his tuition at a state college. The questioning had been brief, simply because the boy had a logical explanation for his presence near the river: he'd been waiting for a girl. The girl, brought in later, corroborated his story. He also had alibis for the killings. He was barely eighteen—how could he possibly be a serial killer, anyway?

Jake escorted Derek Larrington to the door of headquarters after the questioning. The boy kept up a constant chatter, as if on a high, after the interrogation. Or perhaps his nervousness was manifesting itself. After a final apology to the boy, Jake watched as he went down the steps and walked briskly away. Something made Jake remain in place as Derek Larrington headed down the street. The sun flashed on the windshields of passing cars but the day remained dismal to the detective. Just before turning the corner, the boy looked over his shoulder, not directly at Jake but at the police building itself. A smile brightened his face. More than a smile, it seemed to Jake, a smirk of self-satisfaction with a hint of mischief in it. Or malice. Jake Proctor shivered a bit, despite the day's heat. As the boy disappeared around the corner, Jake curbed an impulse to chase him down to ask him: *Why did you smile like that?* Then: *Forget it.* Three experts had questioned the boy, and he had alibis, as well as the girl backing his story. But alibis could be manufactured and witnesses coerced, couldn't they? *Stop it,* he told himself, caught in a spin of emotions. Was he allowing his pain and anguish to affect his judgement, a distant malicious smile to warp his instincts?

Twenty years later he witnessed another clean-cut, well-mannered boy being questioned about murder. This time, the suspect readily admitted killing his mother and step-father. He told his story in straightforward fashion, matter-of-factly. He answered all the questions politely, as if eager to assist the police in their investigation.

Jake Proctor studied Eric Poole carefully as he displayed the scars on his arm, the bruise that remained from the fracture. Later, as he posed for the cameras, a wistful smile appeared on Eric's face, a smile that told the world he was trying to disguise the pain within him. News photographers could not resist that wan, pitiful smile.

But Jake Proctor saw another kind of smile on Eric's lips after he had been brought back to his cell to await the next day's arraignment. Precautions had been taken against a suicide attempt, the boy stripped of belt, shoe-laces, anything that could be used to harm himself. His movements were observed by a camera mounted in a corner high on the wall of his cell. For some reason, Jake Proctor turned back to the cell after letting the others go on before him. He could not shake the feeling that Eric Poole was not what he seemed to be. All his answers had been too pat, almost as if they had been rehearsed. Glancing into the cell, he saw that Eric had turned his back to the camera, was holding his face in his hands, cupping his chin with his fingers. And he was smiling—that same smirk of satisfaction he had observed on that other boy's face so long ago. A smile of secret triumph, as if he had played a trick on the entire world and was enjoying it now in solitude.

Jake Proctor went to the files, brought up on the computer the case of Laura Andersun, whose body had been found in woods near a mall less than three miles from Eric Poole's home. Another file disclosed a girl by the name of Betty Ann Tersa, visiting locally from Los Angeles, reported missing three months ago. Despite the burns and the fractured arm, there'd been no doubt that Eric Poole had murdered his mother and stepfather in cold blood. No remorse had appeared in his eyes as he admitted to the crime. Were Laura Andersun's murder and Betty Ann Tersa's disappearance mere coincidences?

Thus began Jake Proctor's investigation and later his visits to the youth facility where Eric had been sent after appearing in court as a juvenile. All Jake Proctor's experience and observations convinced him that Eric Poole was a serial killer, like an evil incarnation of that long-ago killer of those five children back in Oregon. The old cop did not believe in reincarnation but he believed his instincts and vowed silently to put an end to Eric Poole's grotesque career one way or another.

The ringing of the telephone interrupted his thoughts, and Jake Proctor placed his teacup on the table.

As expected, Pickett was on the line. Jimmy Pickett was young and ambitious, passing his first year in the detective division assigned to Jake Proctor. He'd become the legs of the old cop. He called Jake every morning shortly after seven. To make sure I'm alive, Jake told him. But actually to bring him up to date on overnight reports before Jake left for the office.

"Two more days to go, Lou," Pickett said, using the traditional shortened version of *Lieutenant*. "Think it will happen today?"

"If not today, tomorrow," Jake said. "Or some time."

"Suppose it doesn't?" asked Pickett, a natural worrier whose teenage acne still lingered on his face. "What do we do?"

Jake sighed but his ancient heart kicked in, energized by the thought of Eric Poole as his quarry. "We wait," he said. "Another day, another plan."

Pickett, too, sighed. "Okay," he said, resignation in his voice.

Jake Proctor knew how it was to be young and eager and wanting immediate action, now, at this moment.

"Be patient, Jimmy," he said. "Be patient . . ."

Jake Proctor, old cop, had been patient for twenty years.

Eric Poole did not dream. His sleeping hours were a blank. He closed his eyes at night and plunged instantly into the nothingness of sleep, and woke up just as suddenly, eyes flying open to greet another day, a day without either hope or hopelessness. His three years at the facility had been a procession of such days. Now, only three more remained, and he found it difficult to realize that his freedom was at hand.

He had known at the moment he removed his mother and Harvey from this world that he faced a certain number of years without freedom. He also knew that he was providing himself with protection. Protection from what? From doing what he had done to those three girls, although Lieutenant Proctor, smart as he was, and not as easy to fool as everybody else, thought there were only two. True, he had surprised Eric when he brought up the names of Laura Andersun and Betty Ann Tersa, but the old cop didn't have the slightest knowledge of a girl named Alicia Hunt, who had been the most beautiful of them all.

Eric knew he had been pursuing a dangerous course with the girls, taking too many risks, too often. Finally, he'd found it necessary to call a halt. Temporarily, of course. He enjoyed looking older than his age and could pass easily for seventeen or eighteen. But he also had the disadvantages of being under-age. No driver's licence, no source of income. He knew that he was riding for a fall, certain to trip himself up if he continued on his present course. As a result, the murders of his mother and Harvey would serve several purposes. He'd get rid of a stepfather whom he hated fiercely and a mother who had taken this stranger into their home. He'd also carry out a long-range plan. The plan evolved from news stories in which he learned that the state allowed kids to be tried as juveniles when they committed serious crimes, even murder, if there was evidence of child abuse. Which meant freedom after reaching the age of eighteen. He also became aware of efforts being made to try juveniles as adults for those same crimes. Or to extend juvenile sentences to the age of twenty-one.

Eric saw the logic of carrying out the murders as soon as possible, before the law could be changed. He'd be sacrificing about three years of his life for fifty or sixty later years when he'd be free to do as he pleased.

What a bargain, he sang to himself, as he thought now of Harvey and his mother. Their murders were carried out in business-like fashion, without passion or regret, but he experienced a thrill in his bones when Harvey looked into his eyes at the final moment and realized what was happening. "Goodbye, Harvey," Eric murmured, watching the light of life fading in Harvey's pupils. The moment was without tenderness but had its own special kind of beauty.

After a few months at the facility, Eric was surprised when he experienced longing for the first time in his life, a longing for tenderness made more intense because it was impossible to achieve here.

Although he never dreamed, he spent sweet moments in

his bed, curled up as if in his mother's womb, eyes half-closed, summoning from the past certain moments with his girls—Laura and Betty Ann and Alicia. Moments of intimacy and ecstasy and a piercing tenderness that became an ache within him. But a sweet ache, which he could not resist inviting into the pale thing his life had become. He found that he could interchange the girls in his memory and realized, for the first time, how much they resembled each other, how he was always drawn to girls who were tall and slender, with long dark hair and eyes that contained hidden promises only he could decipher. Alicia had been the most beautiful, tawny skin and thick hair tumbling to her shoulders, hair that made his pulse race and juices fill his mouth. He met her the weekend his mother and Harvey went to the coast of Maine for a brief vacation. Eric convinced them that he should stay home alone, counting on the knowledge that Harvey would prefer not to have Eric accompany them, anyway. Rules and regulations were posted on the refrigerator door, and Eric promised to abide by them. An hour after they left, Eric boarded a bus for Albany, New York, three and a half hours away. Purchasing a ticket required no identification, left no clues behind.

He barely disguised himself, hair slicked back, horn-rimmed glasses he'd bought at a flea market earlier. Wearing the glasses gave him a dim headache and slightly blurred his vision, but the blurring actually softened the harshness of things, blunting the cutting edges of buildings, kerbs, traffic signs, mirrors. In Albany he took a local bus to a town chosen at random because he liked the sound of the name. Haven. He timed his arrival with classes ending at Haven High School. Hung around, spotting at last the girl who turned out to be Alicia Hunt. It had been a simple thing to turn on The Charm, to lure her away from the school bus. She smelled delicious, something lemony and fresh, like long fields at springtime. His fingers trembled as he held her hand and she responded by leaning against him. He enjoyed answering her questions, making up a new, complete history of himself with another name altogether, Carlo Jones, son of a wild and tempestuous mother from South America and a father who was an accountant, of all things. "Oh, Carlo," she had whispered in that secret place to which she brought him, a place where she went to dream her own dreams, away from the world of her everyday life. He had spent a wonderful hour with her as they explored each other with fumbled caresses and passionate kisses. Then those final minutes when he'd been overcome with tenderness. And a sadness, surprising, too, as he thought of Carlo Jones, wondering what it would be like to be someone else and not Eric Poole. Sensing someone nearby, he stilled, listening. The moment passed and he never thought of becoming Carlo Jones again. But he occasionally spent tender moments remembering Alicia Hunt.

He did not indulge in his reveries too often in the facility, knowing the danger of too much desire, knowing that he had to postpone those longings. Instead, he immersed himself in the routine of the place, just as earlier he had adjusted himself to school and home, taking no pleasure in it but accepting the postponement of pleasure. In all the years he spent in the facility, only twice did he come close to achieving moments of tenderness.

The first involved the mouse that began to visit him on a daily basis. He first discovered it after returning to his room following one of the countless workshops. Cute little thing.

His first impulse had been to catch the visitor and dispatch it immediately. The mouse had invaded his private domain and should be executed. But he was also fascinated by the tiny animal. He looked at the furry exterior and imagined its tiny, fragile bones.

It amused him to watch the mouse playing in the corner, small legs skittering as it sniffed the floor, the little rodent nose twitching at the air. He watched it disappear in a hole so tiny he was astonished as the mouse insinuated itself into it. That night, after dinner, he brought a bit of cheese back from the cafeteria, sprinkled broken bits in the corner. In the morning the cheese was gone. He smiled, the flesh of his face feeling strange. Realized he had not smiled in ages. Could not remember the last time he had smiled.

He fed the mouse for the next few days, watched it cavort in the corner, surprised that it did not seem to gain weight. Maybe there was more than one mouse: they all looked alike, of course. The mouse became part of his routine, part of his life. One afternoon it did not show up and he waited. Paced the room. Glanced out the window at nothing. Tried to read but could not. The room seemed to have lost a certain essence that he could not pin down. Then knew suddenly what it was. The room was—lonely. For the first time in his life, he knew what loneliness was like. Until that moment the word had been meaningless to him.

Unaccustomed to such an emotion, he leaped from his chair, wanting to leave, get out of here. But could not, of course. He went to bed that night without carrying out his usual routines: did not do his hundred push-ups, did not read the next chapter in the manual on martial arts he had bought surreptitiously from another prisoner, did not relive one of the bright moments of his life with one of his girls.

Instead, he lay staring up at the ceiling, listening for the sounds of the mouse. But heard nothing.

The mouse returned the next day. He found it nosing around the room when he got back from his last class of the day.

Suddenly, the mouse stood still, as if becoming aware of his presence, stood on its two hind legs, sniffing, quivering nose pointed directly at him. He advanced towards it. The mouse did not move, awaited his coming. He moved stealthily forward, thrilled, recalling how he had moved towards Betty Ann this way. Betty Ann, like the mouse, had had no notion about what was going to happen.

He reached out and snatched the tiny rodent, not surprised that it was so easy. It was as if the mouse knew its fate and was sacrificing itself. The pulse of the small body beat softly against the flesh of Eric's palm. The nose twittered, the body twitched. Despite the loneliness that he knew would be the result of his actions, he gently, lovingly squeezed, seeking the tenderness.

The mouse became still in his hand, the moment of tenderness swift and fleeting, almost non-existent. Disappointed, he slipped the body into his pocket and flushed it down the toilet on his next visit to the bathroom. Felt no regret, felt nothing, as the rushing waters swallowed the mouse.

The second time he sought the tenderness in the facility had been a complete failure. He had also placed himself in a risky situation. The incident involved the bully called Sonny Boy.

There was always a bully on the premises, no matter where you went. Bullies in the school yard, in the school corridors, on the athletic fields. Bullies, too, in the facility, because bullies have a way of eventually screwing up. Bullies came in all shapes and sizes.

Sonny Boy was thin, with pale skin and mild blue eyes. At fifteen, he was already a career criminal. But soft crimes, petty. Shoplifting, housebreaks, auto theft, although he was hardly tall enough to peer over a car's steering wheel. He had finally been sent to the facility for attacking a teacher in sudden fury, holding a knife to the teacher's throat. Eric heard the stories being passed around about Sonny Boy and shook his head in contempt.

Sonny Boy's cruelties were sly and slippery. Jostling, pushing, tripping. And intimidating, of course. All out of sight of the guards. Like all bullies, he had a gift for seeking out likely victims. As if a radar beam zoomed out of his eyes and focused on a target.

Eric, observing at a distance as always, waited for Sonny Boy to find his victim. Just as bullies could be found everywhere, so could the victims. Some were obvious, could have been wearing KICK ME signs on their backs. Eric could name any of a dozen guys who fitted the requirement of victim. He was surprised at Sonny Boy's choice: Sweet Lefty Stanton, an affable, carefree kid who was the star pitcher on the facility's baseball team, easygoing, quick to laugh at a joke, relaxed at all times. The least likely victim in the place because he stood over six feet tall and registered 180 pounds when he stepped on the scales. He spoke in a slow, unhurried drawl.

Sonny Boy had evidently found a weakness, a vulnerable spot in Sweet Lefty's character, because the slow-talking ballplayer submitted himself to Sonny Boy's tricks and ruses.

Still affable and easygoing, Sweet Lefty continued to win ball games as the team's top pitcher and smiled modestly at the applause and approbation. But Eric observed a shadow crossing his face when Sonny Boy approached, saw his meek acceptance of Sonny Boy's jokes and jibes. "You sound stupid when you open your mouth to speak, small brain." He ran errands for Sonny Boy, returned his soiled dishes and utensils to the counter at mealtimes. Remained silent when Sonny Boy ordered, "Shut up."

Everyone accepted the situation without comment or intervention. You did not interfere with the actions of others, no matter how cruel or vindictive. Keep your distance. Don't fight anyone else's battles. Don't even be curious about other prisoners, what they do and why they do it.

His dislike of Sonny Boy tempted him to intervene, to use his reputation as a killer to intimidate the bully. But time ruled out any action. The calendar in his room had shown that less than a month remained before his freedom arrived. It would be stupid to become involved in someone else's problem at this particular moment.

Then: enter the Señorita. Who awakened all his desires and made him ache with his old longings.

The facility was a co-ed institution, but males and females were not allowed contact with each other. According to the rules, that is. They shared the same cafeteria and gymnasium and athletic field, but never simultaneously. They caught swift glimpses of each other on occasion, and the males were quick to call out to the girls, yelling obscenities or variations on what they would like to do to their female counterparts, in language that made Eric turn away in disgust. The raw language of the facility offended him. He did not use such words himself. Harvey, as bad as he was, had never sworn, and his mother had blessed herself whenever she heard anyone using swear words, especially that word beginning with *F*. The *F* word was as commonly used in the facility as salt and pepper on the dinner table. Eric had never used the *F* word.

Prisoners at the facility learned to eat quickly, because mealtime sessions were only forty-five minutes long. Males first, females second. A fifteen-minute interval between the two sessions allowed the cafeteria to be cleaned up and prepared for the arrival of the girls. Eric supervised the prisoners who cleared the tables, wiped them clean, and swept the floor.

Eric saw the Señorita for the first time at the end of the clean-up duties. He was about to leave after a final check of the job when the door to the female side opened unexpectedly and a girl walked in. She was tall and slender, long black hair cascading to her shoulders. Their eyes met and held.

Until the guard's voice intervened: "Hey you, out."

She blushed furiously, which deepened the beauty of her dusky skin.

"My first day here," she apologized, a gentle accent softening her words.

As the guard waved her away, her eyes sought Eric once more. A pang tore at his heart, longing overwhelmed him. Did he see longing in her eyes as well? He found Sonny Boy at his side, leering: "Hey, the Ice Man's falling in love." Eric gave him a withering look and Sonny Boy faded away. Eric realized for the first time that he had picked up a nickname like everyone else: Ice Man.

That night her face appeared before him when he closed his eyes. That low sultry voice echoed in his ears. Even in the drab facility uniform, she had been vibrant in her beauty, a contrast to the other girls in the place. She made him nostalgic for places he'd never known, calling to his mind sun-baked squares, cobble-stoned courtyards, a hacienda sleeping in the shadows. That was the moment she became the Señorita for him.

He caught sight of her occasionally in the next few days, glimpses from his window as she strolled to the ball field, as she left the gym, always the last one to depart. He lingered in the cafeteria after the clean-up, hoping to see her again. Once or twice she entered but always with a group of girls, although she looked his way once in a while and their eyes spoke to each other. He turned away, the pulse in his temple beating wildly.

The old longings were more intense than ever before. He tossed in his bed at night, spent restless moments pacing his cell. He was scheduled to be released soon. But how long would she be a prisoner here? He hoped it would not be long—sentences could be as short as a few weeks, even less if a prisoner was simply awaiting an appearance in court.

He pondered taking steps to get in touch with her. Communication between prisoners was always possible through a system of messages left at certain locations, like the cafeteria or the gym. A trustee known as the Distributor collected and delivered messages. For a price, of course. The price was whatever prisoners could afford, money or cigarettes or an exchange of merchandise, like porno magazines or jewellery. The Distributor was quick-talking and quick-walking, everything about him quick, especially his hands while making the exchanges. He also could arrange furtive meetings, although these were risky, with prices few prisoners could afford, and tough disciplinary action if discovered.

Although he still did not dream, he'd wake up suddenly, his mind full of the sight of her—that long hair, the slim, slender throat. He'd feel his fingers trembling, as if from an old disease. He knew the disease, sweet and precious, that had been muted and slumbering these past three years. He resisted, however, the thought of communicating with her. He was afraid of what would happen if they met, even in this place. And his long-range plans would fall apart. *Patience,* he told himself, *patience.*

His patience ran out three days later. He'd crossed off another day on the calendar, nine days remaining in his sentence. Stepping out of his room, he was startled to see Sonny Boy standing at the end of the corridor. Prisoners were free to wander the hallways and recreation areas at certain times of the day, but no one ever came near Eric. He discouraged visitors, always kept himself aloof, turned off gestures of friendship with a cold, calculating look.

Sonny Boy stood alone down near the red exit sign, his back to Eric, the door half-opened, his shoulders hunched forward as he looked outside. Was Sonny Boy spying on someone? Or waiting for another prisoner to come along? A secret rendezvous?

Fingers trembling, Eric glided cautiously towards Sonny Boy, his sneakers noiseless on the hardwood floor. Was tenderness possible with someone other than a girl? Could the need that kept him awake at night be fulfilled in another way? *Crazy, crazy,* he told himself as he approached Sonny Boy. *I won't do it.* But kept getting closer, closer.

Eric was upon Sonny Boy the way a cat pounces on a mouse. Hands around his throat, the smell of Sonny Boy, sweat and aftershave in his nostrils. Although Sonny Boy was small and thin, he showed surprising strength as he squirmed and struggled, twisting and turning, the strange sounds of survival coming from his throat. Yet Eric took his time, letting him struggle, exulting in this contact, at last, with flesh and bone.

As Sonny Boy went limp in his arms, Eric realized the futility of what he was doing. There was no intimacy in this act, no tenderness at all. The horror of what would happen to him if Sonny Boy should die swept over him as he looked down at the boy's still face. Relieved, he saw his eyes fluttering a bit. He placed his hand over Sonny Boy's eyes, knew that he could not let himself be identified.

As Sonny Boy began to struggle again, trying to rise to his feet, letting out a stream of the swear words Eric hated, that terrible *F* word flying out with spittle from his mouth, Eric found a way out of this situation. "Leave Sweet Lefty alone," he whispered into Sonny Boy's ear. Repeated the words so that there would be no mistaking them. "Leave Sweet Lefty alone." A stroke of genius, Eric told himself, providing a motive for the attack other than the real one. "Understand?" Eric asked, voice hoarse and strained.

Sonny Boy nodded, then went limp once more in Eric's arms. Eric cradled him gently. Looked around: no one in sight. He closed the door. He checked Sonny Boy's pulse, gratified to feel its feeble movement.

There were no repercussions from the assault. Business as usual in the classrooms, at mealtimes in the cafeteria, the athletic field and gym. Eric saw the Señorita two days in succession but she did not look his way. He noticed that Sonny Boy and Sweet Lefty did not come into contact with each other, sat at different tables at mealtimes. At the end of the midday meal three days later, he saw Sonny Boy summon a fat, slow-moving kid called the Bulk to his table. He indicated that the Bulk should return his tray to the service table. Which the Bulk did eagerly, moving quickly despite the weight he carried.

The next day, Sweet Lefty Stanton brushed by Eric as they walked to the cafeteria. "I owe you one, Ice Man," he drawled.

Watch your step.

That's what Sweet Lefty had written in the note. Payback time. Eric thought immediately of Lieutenant Proctor, knowing now why he had not accepted Friday as the day of Eric's release. Because he intended to prevent Eric from leaving.

Eric looked at the calendar. Three days to go. Three days to get through, to be on his guard. He had memorized Sweet Lefty's note, and he ran the words through his mind. *Don't be provoked.* Which meant someone would try to provoke him. His sentence would be extended and his freedom denied if he responded to provocation and got into trouble as a result. If more trouble followed—incidents in a facility could quickly escalate—he could be transferred, when he reached eighteen, to an adult institution. Which meant state prison, a chilling prospect.

At dinnertime that evening, as he stood in line, holding his tray with his utensils on it, he was pushed from behind. A slight push, a nudge. His first instinct was to turn around and push back. But he did neither. The gentle push on his back reverberated throughout his body, reminding him that he had hardly been touched by another person in his years at the facility.

He braced himself, prepared for another nudge, knowing that this is what Sweet Lefty meant by being provoked. Hunching his shoulders, he shuffled forward and received a real push this time, sending him against Dude Man, ahead of him in line. Dude Man turned, staring at Eric in mild disbelief. Dude Man was a sleek and elegant Hispanic, quick to laugh and smile, never in trouble.

"Hey, man," he said. "Whass goin' on? You drunk or somethin'?"

"Sorry," Eric muttered, rearranging the utensils on his tray.

"Thass awright, man," Dude Man said, shrugging, facing forward again.

A push this time caught Eric by surprise with its intensity. A foot was shoved between his legs and sent him crashing to the floor, the tray clattering on the tiles, the utensils scattering away.

Grateful for Sweet Lefty's warning, Eric kept himself in check, curbing his impulse to rise to his feet and strike back at his attacker. Instead, he remained on his knees, reaching for the knife and fork, the spoon out of sight. At that instant he was kicked in the spine, thrown humiliatingly flat on his stomach, sharp pain like an arrow shooting up his back to his neck. He closed his eyes against the pain, sensing guys falling away, not wanting to get involved. On his knees again, he finally looked up at his assailant. A new guy, someone he'd never seen before, a sneer on his lips, pop-eyes bulging from their sockets.

"What's going on here?"

The voice belonged to Dugan, an old guard whose voice still held a hint of Irish brogue.

Eric looked up at him. "I slipped, fell down," he muttered.

Doubt crossed Dugan's face. His eyes narrowed as he looked from Eric to Pop-eyes and back again.

"Well, watch your step," he admonished Eric but looked at Pop-eyes. "I want no trouble here . . ."

As Eric got to his feet, his eyes met the pop-eyes of his attacker. They revealed nothing. His face was a blank, no hate, no dislike, nothing. Like a hired hit man.

Eric fixed the utensils in place on the tray, anger pulsing in his cheeks. He was not really angry at Pop-eyes but at Lieutenant Proctor, whom he knew had engineered the attack. Pop-eyes was merely a puppet. Dugan had stopped the assault, which indicated that the guards were not a part of the plot. Eric was grateful for this. He could handle other prisoners, even an animal like Pop-eyes, but he was not immune to the guards.

As he ate his dinner, isolated as usual, the food tasteless in his mouth, he wondered when the next attempt would happen.

Once again, Sweet Lefty came to the rescue.

He heard a knock on the door of his room just before Lights Out. Leaping to his feet, aware that he had been lying tensely in bed, he placed his ear against the door and heard a muffled voice:

"It's Sweet Lefty."

Turning the knob, he opened the door a crack, apprehensive, wondering if he could trust even Sweet Lefty.

"Tomorrow, at lunchtime. A riot in the cafeteria. Keep out of it . . ."

Eric listened for details but there was only silence, followed by Sweet Lefty's departing footsteps.

He realized he had no choice but to trust Sweet Lefty. Apparently, he still felt he owed Eric a debt.

Later, as he was lying in bed, in the dark, excitement sizzling in his veins, his mind caught fire. How do you keep away from a riot? His days and nights in the facility had been a long succession of routines that had made few demands on either his body or his mind. Now, a problem had arisen and his mind was actually working: probing, analysing. Exhilarated, he pictured the cafeteria, brought up images from old prison movies. Overturned tables, prisoners fighting each other, plates sailing through the air, rushing guards. Then: quarantine, punishment. How do you avoid all that? His thoughts were like pinpricks, keeping him awake, sweet pinpricks as if his brain had come alive after a long slumber.

The next morning during the ten o'clock class in social studies, Eric approached the instructor's desk.

"Asking permission to go to the infirmary," he said to the pipe-smoking teacher, who always wore a tweed jacket as if he taught in a fancy college.

"Not feeling well, Poole?" he asked, his voice also deep and resonant like a professor's.

"Spent half the night with diarrhoea and throwing up," Eric said.

The instructor filled out a permission slip. "Better get it taken care of. You don't want to walk out of here Friday a sick boy."

The infirmary was staffed by a male nurse by the name of Dunstan, who took care of routine cases. Doctors were on call for more serious illnesses or injuries. Dunstan liked pretending that he was a doctor, a stethoscope dangling on his chest. Cheerful, humming, he took Eric's temperature and blood pressure. "All's normal," he announced. He listened sympathetically to Eric's symptoms.

"Take it easy the rest of the day," he said. "Mylanta should do the trick."

Eric pretended to stagger as he stood up, reaching out to the wall for support.

Dunstan, concerned, asked, "What's the matter?"

"Dizzy," Eric said.

Dunstan studied him closely. "Okay, why not lie down for a while? You probably don't want lunch, anyway. Stay here awhile . . . I'll keep an eye on you . . ."

Wonderful, Eric thought, as he made his way shakily to a bed near the window.

"You're probably dehydrated," Dunstan said. "I'll keep you supplied with liquids . . ."

Eric let himself carefully down on the bed, exaggerating his actions, but careful not to overact, keeping a delicate balance.

"I'll be right here if you need anything," Dunstan said, in his best bedside manner, handing Eric a glass of water.

Eric gave himself up to the luxury of relaxation. He knew that if he survived today without incident, he would have defeated the old cop's plans to keep him incarcerated indefinitely. Tomorrow, his routines of departure, exit interviews, a hundred forms to fill out, all of the activity under the supervision of guards and facility officials. The old cop would be foolish to try anything on the final day.

Eyes half-closed, Eric watched the big clock on the wall, tracing the progress of the second hand. Two other prisoners came in for treatment. Eric shut them out, using his old method of removing himself from the scene, isolating himself from his surroundings. Except for the clock.

The clock reached noon, and Eric raised himself on one elbow, breathless with anticipation. A minute passed, two.

As Dunstan approached with another glass of water, the sound of the siren filled the air, a frantic howl that caused Dunstan to stumble, spilling water on the floor. The floor seemed to tremble, bottles rattled on the shelves.

Failed again, Lieutenant, Eric said silently, settling back in bed, the siren like a crazy symphony. He turned away from Dunstan, hiding the smile of triumph on his face.

That evening, after dinner, the Distributor handed him a note.

Still on guard, Eric shot him a questioning look: *Who's it from?*

"I don't know," the Distributor said. "It was in the usual place. I always collect at the receiving end." Fast-talking as usual. His hard face softened. "No charge. A going-away present . . ."

Eric nodded his appreciation, flustered a bit, unaccustomed to accepting favours that weren't earned.

In his room he unfolded the note. Delicate handwriting, blue ink, the paper faintly scented. Without salutation, the note read:

I saw you looking at me. I was looking at you, too. My name is Maria Valdez. I live in Barton, I'm out of here soon. Call me. I'll be waiting.

Her telephone number followed.

He drew the envelope across his nostrils, inhaling the faint scent he could not identify but that smelled beautifully feminine. He pressed his lips against the paper, seeking whatever tenderness it contained. Her long black hair and slender throat came to his mind.

Although he knew the risk of retaining something that could become evidence, he could not make himself throw the note away. He folded it as small as possible and slipped it into his wallet.

At the window, he stretched out his arms, raised his head high, arching his back. In twenty-four hours he would be free.

Free. To follow his destiny. To pursue them all.

Here is why I am fixated on that face and those eyes of Eric Poole on television.

Two days after my twelfth birthday, I was wandering lonely as a cloud like in a poem we read in English, out at the railroad tracks, thinking about my birthday and how my mother arrived home late because she got involved with some guy at a bar and drank too much and forgot to buy the birthday cake.

Then I told myself: *Snap out of it. A birthday cake is not a big thing any more. You are no longer a child but almost a teenager.* A cake was too sweet, anyway, and I was outgrowing sweet stuff, having a taste lately for cheese and redskin peanuts and potato chips instead of chocolate, which I used to crave all the time. So, at twelve, I should not have been sad about not having a cake, and as far as a birthday present goes, my mother would suddenly remember and be full of regret and shame and would buy me something spectacular on payday.

We were living that summer in a small town in New York State and I hadn't made friends with anyone because my mother said her job at a resort restaurant was temporary and we'd be moving again soon. As I walked on the rails, balancing myself precariously, I looked up and saw a guy and girl walking beside the tracks, ahead of me. They were holding hands. They stopped once and he kissed her, gathering her into his arms. Then they disappeared into the woods.

I followed the tracks all the way into town and passed time wandering a mall of discount stores and places to buy fishing gear. On the way back, I paused at an abandoned railroad shack and suddenly he was there, the guy who'd been with the girl, and he was looking at me, one hand in his pocket and the other smoothing out his blond hair.

He was a neat dresser, not sloppy like the usual kids with their baggy clothes. I kept walking on the rail, getting closer to him, and he smiled as if admiring my skill at balancing. Which was silly, of course, but I loved his smile, which made his eyes seem like they were dancing. His eyes were blue like the surface of a pond with the sun shining on it.

"Hi," he said, in a careless voice like he was throwing the word away.

I didn't reply but smiled back at him, my smile matching his, as if we were suddenly connected.

"What's your name, miss?"

Miss. Not *kid.*

"Lori."

"Nice name." A funny expression on his face now, studying me, as if trying to memorize my features.

"How old are you, Lori?"

"Twelve. I was eleven years old only three days ago."

"Happy birthday."

Still smiling but his eyes inspecting me now, from top to bottom and top again.

"Did you get a lot of presents?" As if he was not really interested but only being polite.

"All kinds of stuff," I said. "My mother is a nut about birthdays. She always goes overboard. A big cake and candles to blow out. One year she hired a clown to perform at my party, another we celebrated at McDonald's with all the kids in the neighbourhood."

I was talking fast because I was lying, of course. If you talk fast, it's easier to lie. And I always liked lying because you can let your imagination go and don't have to stick with the facts.

His smile changed, became softer, with a kind of sadness in it.

"Didn't you get any presents at all? Didn't you have a cake at least?" His voice gentle, tender.

At that moment, I thought, *He knows me, he can see right into my soul*, and I felt as if we had been friends for a long time.

"I don't need a cake, anyway," I said. "That's for little kids. I used to like cakes once but not any more. I'd just as soon have a bag of peanuts."

He just kept looking at me.

"My mother is very nice," I said. "She loves me very much. She just gets forgetful once in a while."

He shrugged my words away, lifting his shoulders, and a lock of blond hair fell across his forehead. He pushed it back in place with long, beautiful fingers.

"You shouldn't be out here all by yourself," he said. "What are you doing here, anyway?" As if suddenly angry with my presence.

"It's a short cut."

I almost told him I was wandering lonely as a cloud, thinking that he might understand. Instead, I said, "What are *you* doing here?"

I was about to ask him about the girl when the roar of motorcycle engines burst through the air, coming at us as if we were under attack, dust kicking up, brakes screeching.

Five or six bikes pulled up and surrounded us, the riders with leather jackets and brass studs, dark glasses hiding their eyes.

"Hey, little girl," one of them called to me, a rider with red shaggy hair leaking out of his helmet.

Their engines purred now, the bikes slanted, bikers' legs angled on the dirt, dust settling, the bikes like mechanical horses under them, straining to gallop away.

A biker with a tattoo of a coiled snake on his arm leaned away from his handlebars and reached for me, his glove black and gleaming with brass knuckles.

"Leave her alone," the guy called out.

The bikers turned their attention to him.

The guy was outnumbered and he looked frail and vulnerable standing alone, but his eyes were hard now and not shining but glittering and his chin was firm and his lips thin against his teeth.

The biker with the shaggy hair squinted at him and spat something brown and juicy on to the dirt.

"We was just fooling around," he said. "We got better things to do . . ."

He lifted his hand, signalling to the others, and stepped down hard on the pedal, the motorcycle bucking under him, the front wheel leaping in the air.

"Let's go," he bellowed, his voice hoarse and rough but clear above the roaring of the engines.

More dust raised, as if a bomb had exploded, engines booming, war cries and yelps, and away they went, kicking up dirt, whooping and hollering.

As the dust settled, I began to cough, my throat dry and scratchy. I looked at him through the dust, like a brown mist, wanting to tell him that he'd been very brave. Gallant, in fact. I loved *gallant*, an old-fashioned word that you only see in books.

"Better get going, Lori," he said. "Before something else happens."

His words and his voice stopped me and I did not move. Probably could not move. Because his eyes were not dancing any more and the gentleness, the sadness were back in them.

"What else could happen?" I asked, wanting to add, *I'm safe with you. How could anything else happen?*

"Get going," he said, dismissing me, as if no longer interested, discarding me like a used Kleenex.

He turned away, flexing his fingers, then slapping them against his thighs, as if his fingers were apart from his body and he had no control over them. "You shouldn't come out in the woods like this," he said, scolding, as he looked over his shoulder at me.

I started walking away, feeling more lonely than ever, lonelier even than a cloud, as if I had lost something dear to me that I would never find again.

After a few paces, I stopped and looked back, but he was gone and the spot where he had been standing was a lonesome place.

I ran all the way home, like the little piggy in the nursery rhyme, not crying *wee-wee-wee* but hot tears on my cheeks, anyway.

Now those eyes of Eric Poole on television have caught and trapped me and I know that I must stay in Wickburg and track him down and end this new fixation the way I ended my fixation with Throb.

Remembering that day by the railroad tracks, I know that this fixation on Eric Poole is more than that, it's as if we made a connection that was broken when the bikers came, and that we must meet again. He was so gallant when he stood against the bikers that day, protecting me like a knight without armour.

I close the door of the diner, leaving behind the smell of fried food and the harsh white lights and the giggling of the girls, and I step out into the streets of Wickburg.

Wickburg is like coming home again because my mother and I lived here for almost three years, the longest we ever stayed in one place.

We lived on the third floor of the three-decker on The Hill, looking down on the city. I didn't have any best friends in Wickburg but a gang of older guys and girls let me follow them around if I kept my distance and my mouth shut. The reason they didn't mind my company is because they'd send me into stores to cop stuff for them. I was successful at copping stuff because I looked sweet and innocent, Rory Adams said. Rory was the leader of the gang. He was tall and good-looking.

Rory said I should go to Hollywood and be a child star and grow up to be another Marilyn Monroe. The gang was like a family, with Rory almost a father to us all. A small plump girl named Crystal absolutely adored him, ready to do his slightest bidding. Bantam, a skinny runt of a kid who pretended to be tough, acted like Rory's bodyguard, always walking ahead of us, like he was scouting the territory, clearing the way for Rory.

Anyway, Rory and the gang taught me about living on the

streets, the safe places and the bad places, taught me how to break into locked cars, showed me that secret doorway for the ConCentre stars, and told me about Harmony House. That's my destination as I walk through the twilight streets of Wickburg as the sun disappears behind the city's jagged skyline.

Harmony House is where pregnant teenagers end up when they have no place else to go. They don't yell at you or preach to you there. In fact, they make you feel special. I heard all this when Crystal became pregnant and was thrown out of her house by her father, who realized he couldn't beat her up any more in her condition. After she had the baby and gave it up for adoption—she never told us whether it was a boy or a girl—she described how wonderful she was treated at Harmony House, and I sat on the edges of the gang, thinking about that baby and about Crystal and vowing that I would never give up my baby if I ever had one. But I also felt bad for Crystal. She always looked as if someone was about to hit her when she did something stupid like flirting with the new young cop on the beat, which called his attention to the gang. But Rory never hit her hard, just a slap or two.

I make my way towards Harmony House, hurrying against the descending darkness. I have enough money to stay in one of the motels on Lower Main but I don't want to spend money unnecessarily and those motels are seedy and run-down looking. Places like the Marriott and Sheraton are off-limits because I don't have a suitcase and do not look at all like a career girl. I look exactly like what I am: a runaway.

I can fake it easily for a night or two at Harmony House. There would not be a physical examination right away, and I can make a quick getaway before that happens.

A woman opens the door a minute or two after I ring the

doorbell. She has grey hair like a grandmother but a young, sweet face and it's hard to tell how old she is.

"Welcome to Harmony House," she says. As she leads me to an office off the main hallway, she tells me that her name is Phyllis Kentall and that I can call her Phyllis, all the girls do. She sits at a desk and writes down my name and address, which I fake, of course. I always use the name Brittany Allison when I go on the road and have a card made out in that name, the kind of card that comes in a wallet you buy. She smiles at me and her teeth are white and glossy, like her string of pearls.

"You look hot and tired, Brittany," she says, closing the book. "I'll take you upstairs, where you can bathe" — such a nice, soothing word — "and then you can come down and join the other girls in the television room."

She touches my elbow as we leave the office and pats my shoulder as she leaves me at the door to my room. Handing me a key, she warns, "Keep your room locked at all times. The girls here are very nice, but it's better to be safe than sorry."

The room is neat and plain, venetian blinds on the window and a white bedspread and no rug on the floor. I fill the bathtub and soak in the warm water, thinking of the long day, from the time I hitched a ride with Mr Walter Clayton to that terrible kiss with Throb, and I tell myself I must find an envelope and send the credit cards and licence back to Mr Clayton. In the bed, I fall asleep so suddenly that it's like somebody turned off the lights in my mind.

Nobody wakes me the next morning, and I sleep until almost ten o'clock. Downstairs in the kitchen, a plump, pleasant woman introduces herself as Mrs Hornsby and pours me a glass of milk and fixes me a bowl of Special K. I prefer doughnuts and coffee for breakfast but thank her anyway. She hums as she keeps busy, although she does not look like she belongs there. The kitchen is all glass and stainless steel, and Mrs Hornsby wears a yellow apron decorated with daisies and bustles around like she is a mother of a bunch of small children instead of a cook for pregnant teenagers.

Later, I wander into the large living-room and meet three girls in various stages of pregnancy. Chantelle, Tiffany and Debbie. Chantelle's stomach is enormous, and she sits with her legs spread out and her face, the colour of the mahogany piano in the corner, is moist with perspiration as she lifts a hand in greeting, as if every movement is an effort. Tiffany does not look pregnant—she's tiny and dark, with delicate features like a figurine in a gift shop, and I wonder if she is faking it, too, like me. Her eyes inspect me coolly—does she suspect I'm also a fake? Debbie is so huge that she probably *always* looks pregnant, and her smile is as wide as a doorway.

They are watching an old *I Love Lucy* on television, and turn back to Lucy dressed up as a bag lady as soon as we introduce ourselves. Miss Kentall joins us, and after Lucy has managed to calm Desi down at the end of the programme, she beckons me to follow her into her office. She seats herself behind her desk, looks at me for a few heartbeats, then says:

"You're not pregnant, are you, Brittany? I can tell, you know. A pregnant girl has an air about her. You're a very sweet person, but definitely not pregnant."

"That's right," I say, the colour warm in my cheeks.

"And your name's not Brittany, either, is it?"

I nod my head. There is a time to lie and a time to tell the truth, and Miss Kentall is too smart and wise for me to keep on pretending.

"You're a runaway, aren't you?"

I let my silence provide the answer.

"What's your name?" she asks.

"Lori."

I don't tell her my family name because I want to remain anonymous, which is the only way I can keep my freedom, even in Harmony House.

"How old are you, Lori?"

"Fifteen."

"Why did you run away?" Before I can answer, she asks, "Did you run away from an abuse situation?"

Her voice is gentle, and I realize that she's trying to make it easier for me to tell my story.

I tell her about my mother and Gary and how Gary is a nice guy, good to my mother, and how he touched me on top but very tenderly and how I was afraid that something would happen to hurt my mother and spoil it all for her.

"Your mother must be worried," she says.

"I left her a note. She thinks I'm staying with friends here in Wickburg. We used to live here a while back."

"Have you called her since you arrived?"

I shake my head.

"Don't you think you should call her? Tell her you're safe?"

"I was going to call her soon." A kind of lie: I planned to call her sooner or later but later rather than sooner.

"Tell you what, Lori," she says. "If you call your mother, I can let you stay here for a few days. I need someone to help around the place—make the beds, dust and clean—and give Mrs Hornsby a hand in the kitchen. The pregnant girls are not required to help out. I can only pay minimum wages, but you'll have a place to sleep and food to eat."

"Thank you," I say, hoping that my voice conveys how much I appreciate staying at Harmony House. Now I can make it my headquarters while I pursue my fixation on Eric Poole.

PART II

Eric Poole woke as usual, instantly alert, as if his slumbering mind had been impatiently waiting for this moment. He lay in bed, arms straight at his sides, the same position in which he had fallen asleep.

He knew immediately that something was wrong. Not wrong, different. The sun streamed into the room from his left instead of his right. Ruffled white curtains instead of the facility's beige venetian blinds. Paintings on the walls: summer and winter scenes like the kind you see on calendars.

Aromas filled the air, a woman's delicate scent, perfume or soap and, finally, the invading smell of coffee brewing and something in the oven, corn muffins maybe, that Aunt Phoebe baked for him when he visited her as a small boy.

The smells, the white curtains, the pictures on the walls were such a contrast to the bare, antiseptic room of the facility that he was almost dizzy as he sat on the edge of the bed.

In the kitchen he enjoyed the warm corn muffins soaked with melting butter. Sugar and cream in the coffee, almost too sweet after the black acid-tasting coffee of the past three years.

Aunt Phoebe hovered near the table, wearing a fancy white apron, lace at the edges. He concentrated on the food, aware of being watched, unlike the facility, where he'd felt invisible most of the time.

"I'm so glad you're here, Eric," Aunt Phoebe said, pouring more coffee.

She was either a terrific actress or actually happy for his presence in her house. It did not matter which. This house was a place for him to pass the time he needed to prepare himself for what lay ahead.

Last night, after dinner, they had sat down to watch television together. A news report flashed the scene earlier that day when he'd left the facility, crowds greeting his departure, followed by a shot of the house in which they were sitting. *Weird*, he thought, *looking at TV which is looking back at you as you sit there.* An announcer's voice said, "We tried to talk to Phoebe Barns, the aunt with whom Eric Poole will be living, but she refused to comment on how it will feel to have a murd—" She reached for the remote control and could not find it, and by the time she located it, the word *murderer* had long since blazed in the room.

"I'm sorry, Eric," she said, as the tube went dark.

"Don't be sorry, Aunt Phoebe. And don't be afraid. I'd never do anything to hurt you. Or make you sorry you took me in." Trying not to think of Rudy, the canary.

Eric knew that he would never harm Aunt Phoebe. First of all, there would be no tenderness in the act. Second, he would be spelling his own doom if he did such a thing. When he stepped out of the facility yesterday, he had spotted the old lieutenant in a doorway across the street, a solitary figure apart from everyone else: the television crews, the guards, the crowd of people gathering either to support or to protest against his freedom. He knew immediately that he would have to be extra careful, would have to bide his time, would need patience. But he also knew that the lieutenant could not follow him for ever. Other cases would claim his attention. As for the crowd, they would tire of interfering with his life after a while and go back to their own petty, stupid lives. Another big story would come along. An explosion killing innocent people, preferably children, or the assassination of a beloved figure would take the spotlight away from him sooner or later and free him to do what he needed to do.

Meanwhile, the flurry of activity caused by his departure privately amused him as he ducked away from the television cameras and ignored the questions hurled at him as he crossed the sidewalk. He paid no attention to the cries from the crowd and glanced, without expression, at all the signs— WE LOVE U, ERIC . . . DROP DEAD, KILLA—even though they irritated him. He hated words that were purposely misspelled, like *lite* for *light*, *brite* for *bright*, and, of course, *luv* for *love*.

A black car, hired by his Aunt Phoebe, waited for him at the kerb, and a driver in a black suit held the door open for him, as the crowd fell back, giving him room, resigned to the obvious fact that he was not going to talk. A teenage girl with a daisy tattooed above one eye flung herself at him and kissed him on the cheek, throwing him off balance, her perfume strong and sickening. "I love you, Eric," she called, as guards pulled her away, and he wiped moisture from his cheek, relieved that she did not wear lipstick and had not left her mark on him. Before stepping inside the car, he paused and looked at the crowd, ready for this moment he had anticipated for such a long time. The crowd fell silent, and stopped shoving and pushing. He looked around, savouring the moment, the dazzle of sunshine on window-panes, the sweetness of the air as he inhaled. Then he smiled, the sad, wistful smile he had practised before the mirror, the little-boy smile that he knew would appear later on television screens and the front pages of newspapers. A smile for all the stupid people out there with bleeding hearts for killers. Then he slipped into the back seat of the car.

After the driver closed the door, he could not resist glancing out the window at the doorway across the street. The lieutenant was still there, a frail old man who looked as if a gust of wind would blow him away. Eric gave him a short, sharp salute of triumph, then sank back into the seat as the driver pulled away.

Now in Aunt Phoebe's house, he finished breakfast with the last swallow of the sweet coffee, disappointed to realize that somehow he had adapted to the bitter brew of the facility. He looked up at his aunt, really seeing her for the first time since his childhood. She was tall and thin, a combination of sharp angles: jawline, cheekbones, and nose. But her eyes were mild, light blue, and always seemed as if dazzled by light, on the edge of tears.

She had never married, wore fancy dresses and high heels even when she went off to work at Essex Plastics, where she was supervisor of the assembling department. She went to the hairdresser every Friday evening. Bright lipstick, thickly applied, disguised her thin lips. She wore high heels even when she did the housework, and she clicked across the floor in the high heels now as she went to the window in the living-room.

"They're out there again," she called to Eric.

He joined her at the window but was careful to keep out of sight. Three vans, emblazoned with television logos, were parked at the kerb across the street. Thirty or so people, young and old, milled around on the sidewalk, carrying the usual signs. Some of them stared glumly at the house, eyes dull and resentful. Others wore eager expressions, smiled and waved, in the hope probably that Eric was looking out.

A bald-headed man wearing a white T-shirt and jeans stepped out of a television van and aimed a camcorder at the house, focusing finally at the window where Eric and Aunt Phoebe stood. Aware of zoom lenses, Eric drew away and pulled his aunt with him.

"What's the matter with all those people?" Aunt Phoebe said. "Don't they have better things to do?"

"They'll go away after a while," Eric said.

And so will I.

"Come with me, Eric," she said, leading him to the parlour. They sat across from each other, a small strongbox on the coffee table. She reached into the box and pulled out a blue bank book, which she handed to him.

"I deposited the insurance money at First National downtown," she said. "As you know, Eric, I was executor of the estate and also the trustee. The money is in both our names, but it's yours to do with as you please. A bit over fifteen thousand dollars."

He was not surprised. He had come upon the insurance policies a few weeks before dispatching Harvey and his mother.

She handed him three official-looking certificates, saying, "Harvey and your mother had cheque and savings accounts. I invested that money in certificates of deposit. I timed them to mature and be available to you on your release from that awful place. Three certificates—now worth more than three thousand dollars each."

"Thank you, Aunt Phoebe," he said. "I want to share this money with you." Knowing, of course, that she'd refuse the offer.

"Nonsense," she replied, as expected. "I have more than enough. My job pays me handsomely and I have a fine pension plan for my later years. This money is yours to give you a good start in your new life." She seemed to hesitate, pursing the thin lips, looking away from Eric, then looking back.

He knew what was coming.

"What do you expect to do in that new life, Eric?"

He was ready for her.

"I'd like to stay here for the next week or two. Until I pass my driving test. I took lessons at the facility. I want to buy a van and do some camping this summer. I checked out colleges at the facility and hope to enroll in one in the fall. Either Boston or Worcester. Or maybe a community college somewhere in the state. I want to make something of myself."

He smiled, hoping The Charm of the shy smile added sincerity to this little speech he had carefully rehearsed.

"That's just fine, Eric," she said. "It's good to be ambitious. And you can stay with me as long as you wish."

Relief was obvious in her voice, coming from the knowledge that he would not be a permanent guest.

When Aunt Phoebe drove off to work every day, she ignored the crowds across the street. Eric remained inside the house, killing time, watching boring talk shows on television in which transvestites seemed to be the most popular guests, and game shows where people won speedboats they would never use or went into hysterics about winning a new kitchen. After a few days, he did not bother watching any more.

Heat held the house in a suffocating grip. Aunt Phoebe could not stand air-conditioning, or "artificial air," as she called it, saying that it aggravated her sinuses. Eric wandered the rooms as if he were the only living thing in a museum. He opened the windows once in a while to allow fresh air, however hot, into the house.

The street was seldom without some kind of activity, although lulls occurred from time to time. In the first few days, television crews showed up, focused camcorders on the house while newscasters stood before cameras talking into space. He would later see them on the local news. Newspaper people also made regular visits, interviewing some of the spectators, scribbling in their notebooks. They occasionally crossed the street and rang the doorbell. Waited. Rang again. Then gave up. Eric never answered the doorbell or the telephone.

Once in a while, a parade of cars streamed by, horns blowing and brakes squealing. School vacations had begun, and kids either rallied to his cause or protested against his freedom. Eric resented their intrusions, because they kept interest in him alive and their pictures turned up later in the newspaper or on television, brandishing the stupid signs that cancelled each other out. Sometimes, when the street became suddenly deserted, he opened the door and stepped out on the front porch. He'd look with disgust at the debris left behind by the crowds—candy wrappers, McDonald's cups and paper bags, soda-pop cans. *The slobs are taking over the world*, he thought contemptuously.

The *Wickburg Telegram* was deposited at the back door every morning by a carrier he never saw. Boredom led him to read the stories at first—*Teen Murderer Refuses to Talk*. After a while he ignored them, because they were mostly rehashes of earlier stories with nothing new added. He sensed that the publicity was coming to an end when he saw the headline *Is Eric Poole in a New Kind of Prison?* Reading the story that speculated on what his life must be like in his aunt's house—what television shows he watched, what books he might be reading—he realized that the writers were stretching and running out of ideas. Which pleased him.

What the newspeople did not know was that Eric managed to leave the house occasionally. His aunt became a willing conspirator, driving the car while he sat, cramped and crouching on the floor of the back seat, sitting up only when they were out on the highway. They went on shopping excursions in the malls along Route 9. Bought camping equipment and clothes. "Isn't this fun?" Aunt Phoebe asked, picking out an orange shirt that Eric knew he would never wear.

They checked used-car lots for a minivan, Eric wearing a baseball cap with the visor pulled low over his eyes and dark glasses. After three excursions, he found exactly what he was looking for. A nondescript beige minivan, six years old with low mileage. No air-conditioning and a manual shift, not even a radio, but luxuries were not important to him. His aunt placed a deposit on the van while Eric waited in the car. The transaction would be completed when he received his driver's licence.

His big moment each day came with the delivery of mail, when he looked for a letter from the Registry of Motor Vehicles announcing the day and hour of his driving test. He had submitted his application for the test before his release from the facility, having been advised of a two- or three-week waiting period before he'd be notified of his appointment.

He was running out of patience.

*

Suddenly, he had trouble falling asleep at night, tossing and turning in bed, unable to find a comfortable position. His brain and body clashed in an endless battle, visions crowding his mind, keeping him high-noon awake while his body moved restlessly, as if propelled by the visions.

The visions: soft feminine bodies, long black hair flowing to pale shoulders, glimpses of Laura Andersun and Betty Ann Tersa and, finally, the Señorita. Her note blazed in his mind: *Call me. I'll be waiting*, like neon-lit letters.

He sat up in bed, sweating, breathing hard, as if he had just completed one push-up too many. Looked towards the window at a slant of street light to establish his reality in the bedroom. He had never had trouble sleeping before. Always dropped off as soon as he closed his eyes, waking up suddenly in the morning after a dreamless sleep.

He left the bed and went to the window, looked out at the backyard drenched with moonlight, giving everything, bushes and trees and the picket fence, a sheen of silver. The image of the Señorita blossomed in his mind. He wondered what kind of perfume she wore, what other scents emanated from her body. Wondered how her flesh would respond to his touch, whether her skin would be warm or cool or moist with perspiration. Her eyes were dark, but she'd always been too far away from him to know whether they were brown or black. He preferred black, to match the sweet flow of hair to her shoulders. He imagined looking deep into those eyes as he moved his hands across her flesh, fingertips tracing the lovely landscape of her body until he reached . . .

He turned away, did not allow his thoughts to go further, had to escape the agony of desire unfulfilled, unanswered. Danger in these thoughts. Must not think of the Señorita too often. Not yet. He pictured the old lieutenant out there

101

somewhere, in the shadows, around the corner, watching, waiting.

He saw the girl for the first time the next afternoon, a Saturday, his aunt resting after vacuuming the parlour rug, sipping tea as she watched an old movie on television. Bored and restless, as usual, he prowled the rooms, pausing now and then to glance at the TV set. All the women in the movie wore crazy hats and long skirts and smoked endlessly.

At the window, he looked out at the street, dimly angry at himself for giving in to his curiosity. Not curiosity really but merely a desire for distraction. The crowd had thinned to a few stragglers in the heat of the afternoon. No television vans in sight—in fact, TV crews showed up only intermittently now, for which he was grateful.

A sudden movement drew his attention to the big weeping willow tree on the lawn of the house across the street. A girl stood partially obscured by the long, drooping branches that almost reached to the grass. He caught a glimpse of her face peering through the branches. She suddenly stepped out on to the sidewalk, all yellow and gold. Long blonde hair, pale yellow blouse.

Her face evoked a distant memory, just out of reach. Had he seen her before?

He waited for a commercial to interrupt the movie that Aunt Phoebe was watching. Then, hoping the girl would not go away, he asked his aunt if she owned a pair of binoculars.

"I have opera glasses," she said. "I don't know why they call them opera glasses. I've never been to the opera."

She produced the small black binoculars from the dining-room cupboard, and did not ask any questions.

Eric went upstairs to the spare bedroom at the front of the

house. Keeping to the outer edge of the window, he trained the opera glasses on the girl, who still stood in front of the weeping willow. Her blonde hair caught the sunlight. Her legs were tanned, the beige shorts barely reached her thighs. She was pretty, full lips, a girl's face but a woman's body.

As he studied her through the binoculars, she raised her face in his direction, as if offering herself to him. Once again, she evoked a vague memory. He was certain he had seen her before. But where, when?

He lowered the binoculars. Palms wet. The longing for tenderness startled him with its intensity. *What have I been missing all these years?* He had always been proud of his control over his mind and body, stifling his desires and needs. Now, he was unsure of himself. The girl across the street did not attract him like the others—he was drawn to dark-eyed, long-haired girls—but her presence evoked his desires, making his night-time visions of the Señorita and the other girls pale by comparison. He could no longer be satisfied with visions and daydreams.

That night in bed, he tossed and turned again, but this time as if a fever raged in his blood. The old lieutenant's words echoed in his mind. *You are incapable of feeling, Eric.*

If that was true, then what was this agony that denied him sleep and rest?

Suddenly there was less activity on the street, fewer people showed up and those who did became familiar to him, kids on vacation with nothing better to do or senior citizens who also had time on their hands. Once in a while, a television van drove up and spent a few minutes scanning the street or interviewing spectators. A young guy in his twenties, obviously a reporter, with a camera dangling on his chest and pencils in his lapel pocket, spoke to the onlookers. Eric saw him talking to the girl now and then—obviously attracted to her. The girl did not respond to him and walked away. "Good," Eric murmured, for no reason at all.

The telephone did not ring any more. The ringing had jarred him at first, the sound like assaults on his hearing, disruptive after years at the facility in a room without a phone.

The high point of his day continued to be the delivery of mail. The number of letters had dropped off, and the mail consisted mostly of routine bills for his aunt and an occasional letter from a long-time pen pal in Kansas dating back to her high school days. Eric learned to recognize the purple ink and delicate handwriting. He tossed the mail aside with a grimace when the Registry letter did not show up.

He was stunned when he picked up the *Wickburg Telegram* one morning and saw a picture of the girl on the front page. A three-column close-up, in colour, showing her face peering out of the limp branches of the weeping willow. The paragraph that accompanied the photograph read:

> "Miss Anonymous" in the above photo has kept a daily vigil on Webster Avenue, where released murderer Eric Poole, 18, lives with his aunt, Phoebe Barns. The girl will not give her name or address, and only smiles enigmatically in answer to most questions. Asked if she had ever met Eric Poole, she replied with a one-word answer: "Once." She refused to provide details of that meeting.
>
> Poole was released recently from the New England Youth Services Facility, where he was incarcerated for

three years for the murder of his mother and stepfather. His release has touched off controversy across the state and has led to legislative action calling for juveniles charged with violent crimes to be tried as adults and face stiffer penalties.

Once.

The word blazed in Eric's mind, like a flash of doom. Where had she seen him? And why was she being so mysterious about it? That word corroborated his own feeling that he had seen her before, but her face did not emerge from his memory. He was sure that he had not seen her at the facility, which meant that they must have met at least three years ago. Studying her photo, he squinted as if at a painting in a museum. She was probably sixteen or seventeen years old now and would have been much younger if they had met before he was sentenced. Probably had pigtails, freckles. A kid.

He laid the newspaper aside and stood immobile at the kitchen table. The girl represented a threat to all his plans, a threat to his very existence. The picture in the newspaper linked them together in the minds of the public. She was an unknown quantity, and that meant that she could be any number of things coming out of his past to haunt his future.

Angered, frustrated, he crumpled the newspaper in his hands, wanting to destroy the picture, destroy the girl. Then he sighed, placing the page on the table, smoothing the wrinkles. He had to keep the photograph, study it, absorb it into his system. Maybe that way he would remember when they had once met.

That night, he awoke from a sound sleep, surprised to learn from a glance at the digital alarm clock that it was

4:10. Now what? He had never experienced broken sleep before. What had caused him to vault out of a sound sleep?

Sudden knowledge filled his mind.

He knew where he had seen that girl before.

At the railroad tracks.

Years ago.

He remembered, to his horror, exactly the day and the circumstances.

He had just finished with Alicia Hunt. Had laid her down in a thicket near the tracks, waiting for the proper moment to dispose of her body. He had pushed his way through the brush to make certain that he was alone. That's when he encountered the girl, balancing on the rail, looking directly at him, watchfulness in her eyes, as if she had been waiting for him to appear.

How long had she been standing there?

How much had she seen?

She had smiled, a smile impossible to decipher. He remembered talking to her, trying to draw her out. What had they talked about? Something about her birthday. She was twelve years old—no wonder he had not immediately recognized her across the street or in the photograph. He recalled now how his heart accelerated as they talked. Two in one day. Two within a few minutes of each other. Almost too beautiful to resist, despite the risks. But—how could he dispose of two of them? He had plans for Alicia Hunt but not for this unexpected girl. A child, really. Excitement flooded him, however, at the thought of sharing tenderness with a child.

Before he could make a decision, the motorcycle gang roared into view, kicking up dust and dirt, fracturing the intimacy of the moment. One of the cyclists grabbed at the girl, and Eric shouted at him, surprising himself by coming to the girl's defence, made bold by the knowledge of the power he held over life and death. When the bikers had gone, he said goodbye, a bit sadly and reluctantly, to the girl, and sent her on her way, the job of disposing of Alicia Hunt waiting for him in the woods.

But: *Once.*

She had now come out of the past like a ghost. He did not believe in ghosts but he believed that this girl represented a threat.

His old refrain beat through his mind: *I've got to get out of here.*

But he needed the licence first.

It all happened the next day.

He awoke to rain drumming against the window-pane, ending the heat wave, although the heat had become so much a part of his existence that it had ceased to bother him.

Looking out the bedroom window at the rain lashing the picket fence and the wind stirring tree branches, he felt a rising of his spirits. The rain would keep the last of the spectators, the diehards, like the girl, away from the street.

His spirits soared when he checked the mail at mid-morning and found a letter from the Registry of Motor Vehicles. Finally. He opened it carefully, as if there'd be a penalty if he was careless with the envelope.

The time for his driving test: two days from now, ten o'clock in the morning. Aunt Phoebe had promised to take time off to drive him to the Registry and accompany him on the test. They'd carry out their usual acts of deception, although there'd be no need if the rain continued.

He held the notification in his hands, gazing at it lovingly, as if it were a passport to exotic places.

I have to leave Harmony House.

The sound of rain is like small pebbles thrown against the window as I put my stuff into my backpack. I am trying not to make any noise, even though it's one o'clock in the morning and I'm sure everyone's asleep and the rain disguises my movements.

Although they know I'm not pregnant, Chantelle and Debbie have been very nice to me, and Tiffany pretends to be nice. Chantelle says she was relieved to find out that I am not with child—she never uses the word *pregnant* but always *with child*—anyway, she says I look too young and innocent, although she admits that my body isn't exactly a child's.

Miss Kentall has let me carry out my duties at my own pace and gave me enough time off to let me visit Webster Avenue, where Eric Poole is living with his aunt. She showed me how she wanted the beds made, crisp and tight, the proper use of the vacuum cleaner (as if I had never seen one before) and how much soap and bleach to use in the washing machine.

I have tried to call my mother twice, as Miss Kentall stood beside me, but there was no answer. "Send her a postcard," Miss Kentall suggested. That's what I did. I wrote down that I was having a good time staying with Martha and George and hoped she and Gary were fine and that I would be in touch soon. I signed it, *Lots of love*, with *x*s and *o*s.

After my chores were finished in the morning, I was free until dinnertime, when I helped Mrs Hornsby in the kitchen. The rest of the time I spent on Webster Avenue. I'd take my backpack, which contained ham sandwiches, a can of Classic Coke, and two Oreos that Mrs Hornsby prepared for me.

On my first visit to Webster Avenue, I noticed a big weeping willow tree across the street from Eric's aunt's house, which I recognized from television. The tree is so big and old that the branches reach down to the lawn like a giant green mushroom. The size of the crowd surprised me. Television vans. Newscasters and reporters were talking into microphones and cameras. Teenagers paraded on the sidewalk, holding up signs saying WE LUV U, ERIC, while others carried no signs but their faces were grim as they began pushing and shoving the sign carriers. A man in an Indiana Jones kind of hat called for everybody to be quiet for the noon-time news and the crowd fell silent, pulling back, as if part of a scene in a movie or on television, which is exactly what we were. A car filled with more teenagers roared down the street, and a cop stepped out and halted the car as if the street were not public any more but belonged to the newspeople.

The sun beat fiercely down, dizzyingly, and my head began to feel weightless. Nobody paid any attention to me, so I pushed aside the branches and stepped inside the weeping willow tree, like entering a cool cave in another world. The sounds of the street became mute and far away. After a while, I pulled aside the drooping strands and peered outside.

Eric's aunt's house is an ordinary cottage with white

curtains and dark green shutters against the white exterior gleaming in the sunlight. I saw no car in the driveway. My eyes searched the windows, hoping that he might be looking out, but of course he wasn't. Eric Poole was probably reading a book, waiting patiently for everyone to go away. I thought how strange it was that he had been a prisoner in a kind of jail for three years and how he is still a prisoner and not free at all, although he has served his sentence.

My hiding place in the tree became hot and stuffy after a while, and I stepped out to see the television vans driving away. People also began to disperse, and only a few stragglers remained. I stood apart from the others, concentrating on the house, hoping that he would look out at this particular minute and spot me across the street and remember me from that day on the railroad tracks, even though it was almost four years ago and I was just a kid. Yet, except for my body developing, I am not much different. My face is the same and my hair is still blonde and as long as it used to be.

A young reporter, notebook in hand, showed up and began interviewing people, jotting down their comments, the tip of his tongue visible in the corner of his mouth. I stayed out of his way and did not make eye contact with him.

My other visits brought on lonesome feelings as I stood among the media people and the teenagers and senior citizens, both young and old, with time to kill, the kids on vacation from school and the old people probably glad to get away from their television sets for a change. Eric's house always stood silent, with no signs of life, and I wondered if Eric Poole was really inside or off somewhere, laughing at us when he watches the news on television or reads the *Wickburg Telegram*.

The other day I spotted the young reporter getting out of

a car and I stepped inside the weeping willow. I waited a while and then spread the branches apart looking out. Narrowing my eyes in concentration, I saw a movement at an upstairs window, a flash of light or a reflection, and my breath fluttered in my chest. I spread the willow branches wider and focused on the window, as if I could send my thoughts through the hot afternoon air—*it's me, Lori, who you saw near the railroad tracks*—and the lace curtain moved a bit as if disturbed by a small breeze or a hand that had touched it. A sweet shiver went through my bones, and I stepped out of the tree and raised my head, offering my face to him, ignoring the other people on the sidewalk. Did the curtain in the window move again or was this my imagination, my longing for it to happen making my eyes deceive me?

"You're here again."

The voice startled me, and I turned to confront the young reporter.

"My name is Ross Packer," he said. "I'm with the *Wickburg Telegram* doing a feature on the Eric Poole story." He held up his notebook as if offering some kind of proof. A camera dangled on his chest. He is a few years older than I am, freckles across his nose and cheeks and a wisp of a moustache that he's probably growing to make himself look older. "Mind if I ask you a few questions?"

Glancing back at the house, I wondered if Eric was watching me, thinking that I was betraying him to this reporter.

"What's your name?" he asked, getting ready to write in his notebook.

I shook my head.

"I prefer to remain anonymous," I said, proud of coming

up with that particular answer. "I also prefer not to answer any questions." *Prefer*, a word with a lot of class.

"I won't quote you," he said, slipping the notebook into his jacket pocket. "But I would like to find out why you come here every day."

He kept asking questions, like: Do you live in Wickburg? How old are you? Where do you go to school? Stuff like that. I didn't answer. Only smiled. His eyes kept moving over me, and I knew that he was not interested in my answers after all.

Finally: "You're beautiful. Know that?"

Getting to the point.

"Mind if I take your picture?"

My first instinct was to say no, but I realized that maybe this was what I needed. To be noticed, to set myself apart from the other people on the sidewalk. Maybe if Eric saw my picture in the paper, he would remember that day at the railroad tracks.

"Okay," I said. "My picture. But not my name."

"Miss Anonymous," he said, posing me before the weeping willow and adjusting his camera. He did not ask me to smile but started shooting away, murmuring, "good" and "beautiful" and "just one more." I was aware of people looking at me but I kept my eyes on the camera.

"Have you ever met Eric Poole?"

He asked the question so casually as the camera clicked that I said, "Once." Before realizing I had answered.

"When was that?" he asked.

He must have seen the anger in my eyes.

"I really am sorry," he said. "But I have to get a story. My job depends on it. Eric Poole is a mysterious guy and I'm trying to fill in the blank spaces."

"Why don't you leave him alone?" I said. "He's paid his debt to society." Repeating a phrase I'd heard on the radio.

Ross Packer beckoned me away from the others, and we strolled down the street. Speaking confidentially, tilting his head towards me, he said, "There are rumours. That he maybe killed other people. Two young girls . . ."

I thought of Eric Poole and that shy smile and the way he protected me from those bikers.

"That's crazy."

"Maybe. Actually, there's no proof at all. Only suspicions. That's why they're keeping him under surveillance . . ."

Glancing up the street, I saw only the usual observers, teenagers and old people. Even the media vans and cars were gone for the moment.

"Are you making all this up?" I asked, thinking he was only trying to impress me.

"Come with me," he said. I followed him, curious about what he might know about Eric.

At the corner of Webster Avenue and Adams Street, he said, "Don't look now, but there's a brown van down the street. Nondescript, beat-up looking. A surveillance van, the cops. They keep changing their location but keep tabs on him."

As we turned back towards Eric's house, I glanced quickly down the street and saw the van, ugly in colour and appearance.

"I don't believe Eric Poole killed any girls," I said.

"He killed his mother and stepfather. Once a killer, always a killer." Then, looking at me: "At least, that's what some people say." A kind of apology in his voice.

"He was a victim of child abuse," I said. "That's why he did it."

Ross Packer shrugged. "I've got to get back to the paper. Will you be here tomorrow?"

"Maybe," I said. But knowing that I would be back, all right, because my fixation was still strong inside me.

But now I am leaving Harmony House and maybe Wickburg and maybe going back home and giving up my fixation. First of all, most of my money is gone. I returned from Webster Avenue two days ago to find that Walter Clayton's wallet was missing. I only keep a few dollars with me when I go out, and I'd left the wallet in the drawer of the night table. My door had been locked. But it has an old-fashioned keyhole that requires a simple key. I decided not to say anything about the theft because I didn't want to cause trouble and make accusations that would probably backfire on me, although I was sure that Tiffany had stolen the wallet.

Tiffany has been my enemy ever since I arrived at Harmony House. We were going downstairs for dinner one evening and I suddenly found myself falling, thrown off balance, clutching frantically at the banister, feeling awkward and stupid. I thought my foot had somehow become entangled with Tiffany's, until she said, "Sorry," and continued on her way with a wicked smile at me over her shoulder.

Chantelle, who'd been standing down below, took me aside after dinner that evening. "Watch out for Tiffany," she said. "She's jealous, thinks Miss Kentall likes you better. Miss Kentall gives her the run of the place. So be careful . . ."

One afternoon, I opened my backpack in the weeping willow tree and instead of sandwiches found garbage wrapped up in wax paper and a note that said, *You're not wanted at Harmony House.* When I got back from Webster Avenue, I slipped into Miss Kentall's office and checked the black leather register I signed the night I arrived. Tiffany's signature was there and her handwriting matched the writing on the note.

I was determined to keep living here at Harmony House as long as possible and not let Tiffany drive me away. I enjoyed living here. Nobody gets drunk and nobody gets battered. The day my picture appeared in the newspaper, Chantelle and Debbie and Miss Kentall started clapping when I walked into the dining-room, and even Tiffany joined in. Chantelle pinned my picture on the bulletin board in the hallway. "Prettiest girl we ever had in this place," I overheard her saying to Miss Kentall.

But I have to leave before I get into big trouble. Tonight when I returned to my room after watching reruns of *The Dick Van Dyke Show*, I noticed that my bedspread had been rearranged, as if someone had taken it off and put it back on again. Was Tiffany still searching my room, looking for something to steal? I pulled back the bedspread, blanket, and sheet, and found Miss Kentall's black leather register between the mattress and the box spring. As I flipped through the pages, three twenty-dollar bills fell out, fluttering to the floor. I knew immediately what this was all about. The register and the money would be found missing tomorrow, and a search of the house would follow. They'd be found in my room and I'd be accused of theft. Tiffany's final touch.

I waited for everyone to be in their rooms and stole down the stairs to Miss Kentall's office. I replaced the register in the drawer, relieved to find the door unlocked. Then I returned and began to toss my belongings into my backpack.

115

Now I check the digital clock which tells me that it's 1:23 a.m.

I take the change from my pocket and count it. Seventy-eight cents. How far will nine dollars and seventy-eight cents take me?

Thinking of the missing wallet, I realize that poor Walter Clayton will have to get a new driver's licence and new credit cards. Maybe he's already done that. But the pictures of his daughter, Karen, and his son, Kevin, are gone for ever. I vow to write him a letter someday and apologize.

I blink: there are tears in my eyes.

I get mad at myself.

Stop with the self-pity.

My mother always says, "As long as you've got your health and a new day is coming tomorrow, be thankful." Even if she had a black eye.

I have no black eye.

I have almost ten dollars in my pocket.

I have my fixation on Eric Poole.

And the rain has almost stopped.

Putting on my backpack, I whisper goodbye to the room and I am ready to go.

I will slip out of the house and make my way to Webster Avenue and say a silent goodnight to Eric Poole. Who knows? Maybe he will still be awake and look out the window and see me and invite me in.

Who knows what wonderful things might be waiting for me?

Jake Proctor received the call at six thirty-five in the morning.

He had been up half the night, coughing, a summer-time cold that he could not shake, lingering for the past two weeks, low-grade fever and coughing spells that left him shaken and weary. Air-conditioning made it worse, as he went in and out of stores, from chilled places to the outside heat and then into the car, turning on the air-conditioning, producing more coughs and chills.

He stopped going to headquarters for a while, did not want to spread his cold around and, besides, the air-conditioning in the new building was always set on high, arctic breezes stirring the air.

Jimmy Pickett kept in touch every day, reporting from the surveillance vehicle. Surveillance in this case was minimal, because electronic sweeping of the Barns house had been denied. The chief allowed limited use of the vehicle on adjacent streets, mostly to drive plain-clothes officers to the scene. A useless detail, the lieutenant knew, but a bit of activity to mark time until the monster made his move. Which was sure to come, although the chief and the district attorney disagreed.

"Indulge me," Lieutenant Proctor had said.

"Okay," the chief replied, rewarding him for all those years on the job.

Pickett's voice had been excited when the picture of the girl, Miss Anonymous, appeared in the newspaper. Especially that cryptic *once*. Which meant she had met Eric Poole.

"Think we can use her?" Pickett asked.

The lieutenant contemplated the question.

"Find out more about her."

Later that day, Pickett reported that she was living at a home for pregnant girls. "But, get this, not pregnant. A runaway from New Hampshire. Fifteen years old. We could move in. Use her—"

"Let her be," said the old cop. "She's under-age. Let's not place her in jeopardy. We'll follow the original design—"

A coughing spell obliterated Pickett's sigh of disappointment.

At last, the call came at six thirty-five in the morning, bringing him sluggishly out of sleep. He heard the banging of waste barrels in the street as the rubbish collectors did their job.

"Pickett here. I know it's early." Apology in his voice. "Sorry, Lou."

He responded with his usual morning ritual: coughing, clearing his throat, reaching for Kleenex.

"Go ahead," he croaked finally.

"He's on his way. Left his aunt's house twelve minutes ago—"

"Heading where?"

"West on Route Two, just like you said." Paused, sighing. "We still wait, right, Lieutenant?"

"Right," the old cop said, coughing.

Waiting had become a way of life.

PART III

Now in the driver's seat of his minivan, the wheel in his hand, his foot ready to accelerate, he knew his first full sense of freedom since his release from the facility. The windshield clear of dust, the after-rain breeze cool on his face, the motor purring beautifully under the hood, he steered out on to the street and headed towards State Route 2.

Away we go.

He remained cautious, however, a part of him that could never relax, had to remain on guard, alert. He glanced into the rear-view mirror to see if he was being followed. He checked out cars that pulled into the street behind him as he passed.

He was on the lookout for an old beat-up car driving behind him at a discreet distance. As ridiculous as it sounded, he thought that old Lieutenant Proctor would be driving a car as ancient as himself, dusty and used up. Told himself to shrug off that possibility but kept looking, anyway.

He stopped–started at several traffic lights, enjoying the throb of the engine reverberating under his feet, the small vibration of the steering wheel in his hand. He felt the sweet surge of ownership. He rolled up the windows, sealing himself off from the rest of the world.

Finally free of city traffic, he entered the ramp that led to

Route 2 and beyond. He kept his speed under fifty-five, letting other cars pass him by. He did not want to run the risk of speeding—or going too slow—and being pulled over by a cop. Knew he had to maintain a violation-free life. Not call attention to himself. Live by the rules. Appear to live by the rules, that is.

Pulling up at the first rest-stop, he parked facing the highway. And waited. Leaned forward, chin resting on the steering wheel, studying the oncoming vehicles as they approached. Cars whizzed by, most of them obviously going faster than fifty-five. He would have to make adjustments, probably drive at around sixty. He saw nothing suspicious about the traffic. Commuters on their way to jobs in Worcester or Boston, nobody slowing down to check out the rest-stop.

At that precise moment, as he relaxed his grip on the steering wheel, a white car with two men in the front seat slowed down as it approached the rest-stop. Turned in and drove slowly past his van, stopping near a green rubbish barrel, about forty feet away.

Eric stilled as he always did when a threat presented itself. As if his heart had stopped beating, his blood ceasing to flow through his veins and arteries. His senses grew sharper, alert, keen.

Through the rear-view mirror, he saw one of the men vault from the car, stumble towards the woods, falling suddenly to his knees and vomiting violently.

Eric relaxed and took his eyes away from the mirror. No longer stilled, his heart beating again. His legs and arms prickly as his blood began to churn through his body once more.

He drove slowly out of the rest-stop, the place deserted at this time of day, and pulled on to the highway.

He was cruising along at fifty-eight or fifty-nine, keeping to the right-hand lane, when a sound reached his ears, fracturing the silence of the car. What sound? A movement of some kind.

Instantly alert again, he realized he was not alone in the car. Somebody or something in the back seat. Crouched down, hiding, as he himself had hidden when Aunt Phoebe drove him away from the house. He slowed a bit, looking for a place to stop, saw a highway sign warning EMERGENCY STOPPING ONLY. Knew he could not afford to break that particular rule and risk a cop car stopping to offer assistance.

He accelerated slightly, cautioning himself to relax as he saw the starkness of his eyes in the rear-view mirror.

No more movement in the back seat—was his imagination playing tricks?

He spotted a highway sign announcing Exit 22, a half mile away from a place called Hancock. Flashing his turn signal, he drove towards the ramp, entered, rounded a 180-degree curve, and halted at a stop sign. Waited for two cars to pass, then turned right. A quarter of a mile down a street of small houses, with faded paint and unkempt lawns, he came to an abandoned gas station, a huge FOR LEASE sign on the garage door. He pulled into the place, parking alongside an old gasoline pump.

Tensing himself, his voice barely above a whisper, he said, "I know you're there. Who are you—what are you doing in my van?"

Her face popped up in the mirror. The girl across the street, Miss Anonymous in the newspaper. Green eyes gazing at him, like a little kid caught doing something she shouldn't.

"Hello," she said.

We look at each other.

He can't believe his eyes as he looks at me.

And I can't believe I am actually here in his van, looking at him. Can't believe that I slept here in the back seat during the night and drove away with him this morning.

Here's what happened:

Last night, after I left Harmony House, I walked all the way to Webster Avenue in the rain to say goodbye to Eric Poole. He wouldn't know I was saying goodbye, of course. I figured I would visit one last time.

The rain streamed down, penetrating my clothing and plastering my hair to my head, and I didn't care as I stood looking at his house, a night light glowing at the window, all cosy and warm inside. Shivering, I vowed to track down Eric Poole some other time and plant that kiss on his face and end my fixation.

Damn it.

I didn't want to leave Eric Poole while the fixation had me in its grip.

A dog barked at me, a black German shepherd a few feet away. His owner wasn't in sight. I was all alone on a rainy street menaced by a strange dog, his front legs stiff, body arched, wet hair matted against his body as if he was ready to pounce.

I started across the street, the dog following me, still barking. I was determined to ring the doorbell. Eric Poole would open the door, recognize me, and take me in his arms.

Standing at the bottom of the steps, I knew how ridiculous those thoughts were. Dripping wet, shivering, I turned to the dog. "Get the hell out of here."

The dog yelped forlornly, then hung its head.

Desperate, I spotted a minivan in the driveway. Never noticed it before. Maybe it had been parked somewhere in the backyard.

My backpack bouncing heavily behind me, I ran across the lawn, my sneakers squishing on the grass. Arriving at the van, I looked around for the dog. It had not followed me, had wandered off looking for its own shelter, probably.

The van door was locked.

Using the method Rory Adams had taught me, I opened the van door after a few tries, the rain making it harder to do. Slipping inside, I curled up on the back seat, grateful that the driveway was dark. I became part of the darkness, shivered, hugged myself to keep warm, my backpack on the floor, clothes stuck to my body as if the wetness were a kind of glue.

Weary and disgusted, lost and helpless, I listened to the sad sound of the rain on the metal roof and fell asleep.

The sun blazing through the window woke me up. Heat filled the air, stifling in its heaviness. My throat was parched, arms and legs stiff and aching, mouth so dry I could barely swallow. My clothes, still limp, clinging to my skin.

Looking up, starting to yawn, I was horrified to see Eric Poole walking towards the car, swinging a small travelling bag in his hand. He wore a blue shirt, open at the throat, and jeans. I tumbled to the floor on top of my backpack, hoping he'd walk past the van.

The door opened, letting in a burst of fresh air. I held

myself rigid as he slid behind the wheel, the back of the front seat bulging a bit as his body settled in. Would he smell my sweat?

The engine roared into life before settling down to a quiet murmur.

And the van began to back out of the driveway with Eric Poole and me in it.

"You."

Stunned by her presence in the van, he knew immediately the danger she presented. Everything about her spelled danger, taking away the initial surprise at finding her here.

She could be stalking him, intending to confront him about what happened that day at the railroad tracks. The old cop could have set her on his trail.

"I'm sorry," she said. "It was raining last night, and I got in the van and fell asleep."

But the van had been locked.

"Get out," he said. But even as he spoke the words, he knew he could not dismiss her like that, could not abandon her until he found out who she really was and what she knew.

As she scrambled to gather herself, rearranging her clothes and picking up the backpack, he said, "Wait."

She paused, one hand on the door handle, the other on her backpack, regarding him with sudden expectation in her eyes. She was in disarray, her damp blonde hair tangled and all askew, face moist with perspiration, a smudge of dirt on her cheek, wrinkled white blouse. He was also aware of her body under the clothes, her breasts filling the blouse, the outline of a nipple, dark and distinct in the damp cloth.

"Who are you?"

"I ran away from home. It's a long story..." Made a helpless gesture, lifting her hands, her shoulders, as if too weary to talk about it.

"Why were you hiding in my van?"

"I wasn't hiding," she said, pushing a damp lock of hair from her cheek. "I had no place to go. A dog was chasing me." Sweat glistened on her face. "Can you open a window, please? It's hot in here..."

That simple request made her appear to be exactly what she claimed: a homeless girl looking for shelter in the rain. But he could not afford to trust her yet.

"Who sent you?"

Surprise made her flinch, as if he had slapped her face.

"Nobody sent me. I'm on my own." Puzzled. "Who would send me, anyway? I told you: I had no place else to go."

She picked up her backpack. "I'll get out," she said. "I'll go..."

Don't do anything foolish. You can't let her go. She saw you that day.

"Relax."

As he turned away, trying to figure out his next move, he caught a movement in his peripheral vision. A dark blue police cruiser was moving slowly in his direction. HANCOCK POLICE was inscribed on the door in white block letters. Coincidence? Maybe he was being followed, after all. Maybe the Wickburg authorities had been tracking him down, had radioed ahead to towns along Route 2—*Be on the lookout for Eric Poole, travelling with a girl in a beige minivan.*

Tense and stilled, he watched the cruiser advancing, moving so slowly that he expected the engine to buck and stall. A lone cop, with a long, thin face, visor shading his eyes, looked at the van, a long, lingering scrutiny.

This was the moment for the girl to make her move, to leap from the van and claim that Eric had kidnapped her, was holding her against her will, which would send him away, not to the facility this time but to prison. Remembering the malice in Lieutenant Proctor's eyes, he knew that the old cop would not hesitate to frame him, to use this girl as bait in the trap.

He heard the girl drop her backpack to the floor, heard the swish of her thighs as she moved her legs, smelled her sweat, a hint of stale perfume in the smell.

The cop studied the van for another long moment, then directed his eyes towards his windshield. The cruiser rolled on, picking up speed, moving past the service station. The girl had not called for help.

Eric sagged with relief against the steering wheel, then immediately straightened up, did not want the girl to realize how worried he'd been.

"Okay," the girl said. "I'll get out now." She struggled to hoist the backpack over her shoulders. "I'll hitch a ride to the next town."

"Then what?" he asked, almost absently, his mind racing to decide what he should do about her. It was too soon, too risky to do what he might have done without a second thought a few years ago.

Shrugging, she said, "Look, I ran away from home, but now I want to go back. I'll call my mother. She'll come and get me."

She reached for the door handle, but he grabbed her arm, arresting her movement.

Eric knew that he could not let her go. Not now, if ever. She still represented a threat. Sleeping in his van on the night before his departure had to be more than a coincidence. Who had taught her to break into a locked car? Remembering his chance meeting with her that day by the railroad tracks, he wondered why she had appeared in his life at this particular time. All of it added up to one thing—he could not let her go. But had to win her confidence, put her at ease so that she would not be tempted to escape. And maybe he could find out the answers that way.

"Let me help you," he said, making his voice tender, slipping on the old wistful smile.

"Why?" she asked, settling back on the seat.

"Why not?" he said. "Maybe I like your company. Maybe I've been alone too much."

A wan smile appeared on her face, and she looked suddenly like a lost child, grateful for a bit of kindness.

The Charm was still working.

I melt when he looks at me that way.

I feel my legs go all watery, and my stomach almost caves in and my breath comes fast and I can almost feel my top swelling up. I want to kiss him.

Does he know who I am?

You, he said, when he first saw me here in the van.

I wonder if that means he remembers me from that day near the railroad tracks or my picture on the front page of the newspaper.

At first, he was suspicious and a kind of anger smouldered in his eyes. But now I guess he has changed his mind about me and he is suddenly gentle and, yes, almost tender.

"Get in the front seat," he says, but not as if giving an order but inviting me to sit beside him.

I figure that this is the moment to tell him about my fixation and go ahead and kiss him, place my lips on his lips and get it over with.

Before I can decide to do it, he starts the engine and we back up and then pull out into the street, his eyes straight ahead, concentrating hard on his driving. He is careful, cautious, seemed unsure of himself when he shifted gears.

We travel a few miles without speaking.

"Have you had your licence long?" I ask. Not that it really matters but only to make conversation. To fill the silence in the van. More than silence, an emptiness, as if he is sitting here beside me and yet is far away.

"What?" he asks.

Like he did not hear me. Or did not understand what I asked, and I was speaking a foreign language.

"Your licence. Did you just get it?"

"Yes," he said. "Am I a bad driver?" Glancing at me as if my answer is important.

"You're a very good driver." What else would I tell him?

He doesn't say anything for a long time, as if he's thinking over my answer. Then: "Thank you . . ."

I am starved. My stomach is so empty that it begins to rumble, and I am embarrassed by the sound. I check the dashboard. The van does not have a radio. No air-conditioning, either. Windows only for the front-seat passengers. The air coming through the windows is still and old, with a dash of chemical. We are probably driving past a plant of some kind that belches foul stuff from its chimney.

I wonder where we are going, where he is taking me. But I hesitate to ask. I am afraid to ask.

I remember what that reporter told me about the rumours that he had killed two girls.

I remember how tense he became when that cruiser pulled up and the cop looked at us for a few minutes.

Glancing sideways at him, hoping he doesn't catch me doing it, I study his profile, delicate, just a tiny bump on his nose. He is good-looking, all right, but that doesn't mean he can't have killed those girls.

Relax, I tell myself. If he was a killer, he wouldn't have been set free, he wouldn't be running around loose like this.

I see the sign up ahead that says:

GREENHILL PARK
ALL WELCOME

And we turn off the highway into deep, dense woods.

A park was perfect for his purposes. Away from the highway, from cruisers with cops who could stop him at any moment.

He steered the car over a dirt road, concentrating on the twists and turns, trying to keep his mind off the girl but aware of her beside him, and the way she moved on the seat.

He had not been alone with a girl for so long that he did not know what to say or how to act. In fact, he had never actually been alone with a girl for any length of time except for Laura and the others, but those had not been exactly social situations.

His years at the facility had been the teenage years, when he'd have been developing social skills—that's what the instructor had called them during one of the classes. That's why he felt dumb and inadequate questioning the girl. What he needed was time. Time to become more acquainted with her, to find out exactly who she was, what she'd been up to on the street of his aunt's house every day and sleeping last

131

night in his van—to find out if she was really as innocent as she seemed.

He pulled to the side of the rutted road and stopped, the van purring beneath his feet. Waited to see if a car had followed him into the park. The heat gathered quickly in the van. The girl stirred beside him but said nothing.

He made himself wait five minutes, glancing at his watch occasionally. Then started the car, satisfied.

Sweeping around a curve, they arrived at a sudden clearing in the woods. The girl exclaimed: "Wow! This is really nice."

He was struck by the difference between her body, full and ripe as a woman, and the way she sometimes talked like a little girl, awe-struck and full of wonder. Like now, at this moment: "What a neat place."

He nodded in agreement, checking for the presence of a cop or a police cruiser and finding none. After all those years at the facility and then a virtual prisoner in his aunt's house, he had forgotten that places like this existed. A small pond lay before him, its blue surface stirred by a gentle breeze, the ripples like wrinkles on a blue bedspread. Tall pines guarded the pond. A bandstand on the far side, where, he imagined, concerts were held on Sunday afternoons as families gathered. A pavilion with a wide wraparound porch to his right. Dances were probably held there on Saturday nights. He wondered why he felt lonesome suddenly.

"Look," she said, pointing to an area occupied by swings and slides and a small merry-go-round on which two little girls laughed with delight as a woman spun them around. A small boy zoomed head-first down a slide, and his father caught him at the bottom, then swung him high in the air.

As they drove into the park, he saw a teenage couple at

the water's edge, tossing small pieces of bread on the water. White swans, with necks like the porcelain handle of his mother's best china, pecked at the bread and still managed to look graceful.

He drove to a spot where picnic tables had been set up in a pine grove. Parking the van, he waited a moment, hands on the steering wheel, considering his next move. He had to decide what to do about the girl before he contacted the Señorita. The image of Maria Valdez formed in his mind, the long hair, the way she had looked at him across the cafeteria. What pleasures she presented, all within his grasp very soon. But first, the girl.

"Can I get out and stretch my legs?" she asked, startling him, bringing him back sharply to this place, the park, the van in which he sat.

"Why not?" he said, finally. They were surrounded by deep woods, had driven at least a half mile in from the highway. If she tried to flee, he could easily outrun her.

She disembarked from the van, pausing and stretching, her breasts straining against the blouse as she raised her arms. She made her way to a picnic table, pine needles crunching under her sneakers, and sat down, chin in her hands, contemplating the pond. She looked—sad. More sad than scared. A good sign. He wanted her to become comfortable with him.

He sat down across from her. Had to pin her down now, obtain information.

She looked up at him expectantly, waiting, as if knowing that the time had come to answer questions.

He wondered how to begin.

To his surprise, she began for him:

"Don't you remember me?" she asked.

"Why should I remember you?" he countered, cautious, not wanting to admit anything.

Disappointment in her eyes. "That day by the railroad tracks? A long time ago?" Sighed, "Maybe too long ago . . . I was just a kid . . ."

He realized that he had nothing to gain by denying meeting her, that, in fact, he had to find out how much she knew about the events of that day.

"Yes, I remember," he said. "It was around your birthday, wasn't it?"

She smiled, the child in her appearing once again. "That's right. My mother forgot it and you were very nice. We had a good talk. Then the motorcycle guys came along. I thought you were very brave. You told them to leave me alone." Shaking her head in fond remembrance.

"What else do you remember?" he asked. And was immediately angry at himself. The questions might spark a memory that was better left undisturbed.

She shrugged, at ease now, leaning forward, spreading her arms along the table.

"I remember that it was a beautiful day and I felt bad after I ran away from that place. I wanted to go back the next day to see if you were still around. Crazy thought, right? I never got there, though. My mother and I left town that same night. She got a job over in New Hampshire. We always leave places in a hurry . . ."

He bowed his head in grateful relief. She did not remember the girl, could not link him with Alicia Hunt. She didn't represent a threat to him after all.

Sighing, glancing around, she said, "It's beautiful here, isn't it?"

"Yes," he said.

"Know what?"

"What?"

"I'm starving." Looking towards the pavilion.

Following her gaze, he saw an old man wheeling a white pushcart across the park road, stopping at the water's edge. HOT DOGS, ICE-CREAM, POPCORN, announced signs on the side of the wagon. The old man unfurled a candy-striped umbrella that shaded the wagon from the sun.

"You didn't have any breakfast, did you?" he said.

She smiled. "See, you're still being nice, Eric."

Saying his name for the first time. He realized he had not heard his name on a girl's lips since Alicia Hunt. Who smelled of lemons, whose dark hair clung to her cheeks. He tried to picture this girl with dark hair.

They left the picnic grove and strolled by the pond, watching the swans floating like small icebergs as they moved away from the shore, having been abandoned by the teenagers, nowhere in sight now.

Walking beside her, he was convinced of her innocence. He could let her go. Drop her off at the next town, give her enough money if she needed it for the bus fare home, and go on to meet Maria Valdez, the Señorita. Feeling expansive, glancing at her almost with affection. Meanwhile, they could stay here a while. Relax from the heat of the day. Maybe take a swim. He searched the shore, looking for a beach.

"What are you looking for?" she asked. "Is something wrong?"

"No," he said. "I just realized there's no beach here." Realized also how alert she was.

"That's fine with me," she said. "I never learned to swim. Always seemed like there were other things to do."

The young couple who'd been feeding the swans were in a canoe now, gliding lazily on the pond. The girl wore a big white hat and sat languidly at the front of the canoe, her hand trailing in the water.

"Isn't that beautiful?" the girl beside him asked. "That's what I'd like to do some day. Wear a white hat like that and go out in a canoe. My hand in the water." As if talking to herself, had forgotten all about him. "To live the life other people live . . ."

At the concession stand, she ordered two hot dogs, a Klondike bar and a Coke. The old man twirled his white moustache with one hand while he handed over the order with the other. She loaded her hot dogs with mustard and relish but skipped the onions. He was content with a Klondike, still without appetite. Or, rather, he had an appetite for the fresh air, the green of the pine trees, the blue of the pond, the grey of the rocks. As if all the time in the facility he had been colour-blind and his deprived senses had at last awakened after a long sleep.

He drank the air into his lungs as they made their way back to the picnic grove.

She ate voraciously, barely chewing the food before swallowing. He wiped away a dab of mustard on her cheek. She smiled her thanks while chewing. The ice-cream was cool in his mouth and throat.

She guzzled the Coke, burped discreetly, smiled an apology.

"You don't remember my name, do you?"

He side-stepped the question. "I thought you wanted to be anonymous . . ."

"Not with you." She swallowed the last of her Coke. "I told you my name was Lori, which is what everybody calls me but my real name, ugh, is Lorelei. My last name is Cranston. Like the Shadow . . ."

"What shadow?" She had the ability to keep him off balance.

"An old radio show, years ago. But made into a movie a while back. The Shadow knows . . ." she said, in exaggerated accents. "Anyway, the Shadow's really Lamont Cranston, New York playboy. My mother sometimes calls me Shadow when I start driving her crazy, like telling her she shouldn't drink in the morning . . ." Sighing, she said, "But I like *Shadow* better than *Lorelei* and *Lori* best of all."

"I promise never to call you Lorelei, okay?" he said, trying to match her light mood.

"Say it," she said.

"Say what?"

"Lori."

"Okay . . . Lori."

"Okay if I call you Eric? Like I did a few minutes ago?"

He shrugged. "If you want to."

"I want to, Eric." And smiled, illuminating her face, eyes radiantly green, cheeks faintly blushing. If only her hair were black, her skin dusky like his girls'.

Her voice playful, she said, "You haven't asked me why . . ."

"Why what?"

"Why I went to your aunt's street every day . . ."

Caught by surprise, he improvised quickly. "I figured you'd tell me in due time," silently upbraiding himself for overlooking such obvious questions and for not having asked her name, either.

"Don't laugh when I tell you."

"I don't laugh very much," he said, realizing the truth of

the statement as he made it, this sudden bit of knowledge disturbing him.

She took a deep breath. "I am fixated on you," she announced.

"What do you mean, fixated?"

"Like, I get fixated on things once in a while. Not things, really, but people. Like you. When I saw you on television the day you got released, that's when it happened. I remembered how nice you were that time near the railroad tracks, what a nice smile you have, and bang, I got fixated again . . ."

But she hadn't told him what fixated *was*, and he waited.

"Okay," she said, as if suddenly reluctant to provide an explanation. Looking away, blushing slightly, she said, "Fixated means I need to kiss you. But a real kiss, I mean." Pause . . .

". . . our tongues touching . . ."

He didn't know whether to laugh at this preposterous girl or get rid of her as soon as possible.

"I know it sounds ridiculous," she said. "But I can't help these fixations. Just let me kiss you and it'll be over . . ."

He could not kiss this girl. Maybe he could not trust himself to kiss her. Despite her beauty, he was focused on Maria Valdez. Yet a part of him was curious about what might happen if he kissed her, if their tongues actually touched. All these years at the facility without a girl, only memories. Would there be tenderness in the kiss? Would it lead to something else?

"Okay," she said briskly. "Forget it. I shouldn't have mentioned it . . ."

As she raised an arm to touch her hair, he noticed the scars on the inside of her wrist. Remembered similar scars on the wrists of a kid called Carmine at the facility who'd been put on a suicide watch.

He reached for her hand, turned it over to expose the scars.

"Did you try to kill yourself?"

"Maybe. I don't really know," she said, avoiding his eyes. "I didn't want to live but I didn't want to die, either. My mother . . ."

"Did she abuse you?"

"No, my mother has always been good to me. She never hits me. But she's weak, sometimes. Tries to do the right thing, then has another drink and forgets what the right thing is."

"Like forgetting your birthday, right?"

"My wrists had nothing to do with my birthday," she said. "It was stupid, something I'd never do again. I was lonesome. My mother was off on a binge with a guy who liked to slap her around after. My first period came, blood all over me, and cramps. I drank some whiskey left over in a bottle. Took some pills, tranquillizers, I found in the medicine cabinet. Discovered razor blades there, too. Got into the bathtub and looked at all that blood. My mother found me when she got home. Called 911. At the hospital, my cuts didn't heal, a staph infection. That's why the scars are still there . . ."

"I'm sorry," he said, the words surprising him as he spoke them.

"Thank you," she said.

"For what?"

He never knew what to say to this strange girl, careless in the way she moved her body, sexy and innocent at the same time. He had a sense of time being wasted, precious time, with her here at the park. Disturbed, too, that he could not make up his mind about what to do with her. In the days before the facility, he'd always been decisive, with no doubts about his actions or what he must do to the girls, Harvey, his mother. Had his years out of circulation changed him, softened him? He sensed danger to all his plans if that had happened.

"Let's feed the swans," she said, leaping to her feet, as if she had sensed his mood and wanted to dispel it.

He bought a bag of bread crusts from the old man and they tossed them to the swans. Their graceful movements, even as they darted for the food, pleased him.

"Oh," the girl said, her arm raised to throw another crust but the movement arrested, the bread dropping from her hand. "I remember something else about that day."

"What day?"

"By the railroad tracks. The girl . . . you were with a girl that day, remember? I saw you walk into the woods with her. And a while later, you came back out alone. Remember now? That's when you saw me . . ."

He was always at his best at moments like this, calm, languid, but his mind racing, thoughts sharp and clear.

"I remember now," he said. "A girl I'd just met at the mall. She'd lost her wallet taking a short cut through the woods near the tracks. I said I'd help her look for it. We retraced her steps . . ." He was pleased that he had not lost his ability to improvise at short notice.

"Did she find it?"

She had doomed herself by remembering the girl and it didn't matter now whether she was baiting him, playing a role designed by Lieutenant Proctor. She knew about Alicia

Hunt, could link him with her. She had witnessed them together the day Alicia Hunt disappeared. In fact, he realized sadly that Lori Cranston was completely innocent. Not even the lieutenant knew about Alicia Hunt.

"Did she find it?"

Her voice came to him as from a long distance, and he realized she'd had to repeat the question.

"What?"

"Did she find it? Her wallet?"

"No. We looked and looked . . ."

"She wasn't your girlfriend?"

"No, I'd only met her a few minutes before . . ."

Eric was swept by an overwhelming sense of loss, knowing that he must do what he did not want to do. There would be no pleasure ending this girl's life, no tenderness at all. There would be the usual risks. He would have to take extra precautions, be absolutely certain that he wasn't being followed, hadn't been seen at all with her.

Tossing the rest of the bread to the swans, a shower of crusts pebbling the water, he said, "Time to go."

The sooner she died, the better it would be for both of them.

He tried to smile as she turned to look at him.

Why is he looking at me that way?

Almost gives me the shivers, his face suddenly turning to stone, his eyes darkening, and his mouth drawn tight so that his lips become thin and bitter, like lines in a drawing.

Other times, his face is soft and his eyes mild and gentle, and he tilts his head as he looks at me, a kind of wonder in his eyes as if I am a rare specimen he's never encountered before.

141

He doesn't respond to me the way other guys do. I mean, when I move my legs or draw back my shoulders so that my top sticks out—like when I got out of the van and stretched my arms to test him—his eyes passed over me as if I was a mannequin in a store window.

Maybe it's because he has been locked up since he was fifteen years old and has not led a normal life. But I wonder if his life was normal before that. I mean, he killed his mother and stepfather, for goodness' sake. So his life couldn't have been exactly like everyone else's. I've heard about the scars on his body from the times his stepfather abused him and that wasn't normal, either.

He's a puzzle to me.

When he wiped that dab of mustard from my cheek, his touch was tender.

As he held my arm and looked at the scars on my wrists, his grip was firm but his eyes were gentle.

But he lied to me.

And the lie again reminds me of what that reporter said, the rumours that he killed two girls. That's hard to believe. Or maybe it isn't.

The lie gave me shivers.

He said that the girl he walked into the woods with was not his girlfriend, that he had only just met her at the mall and was helping her find her lost wallet.

But I saw them holding hands and then he took her in his arms and kissed her, a deep long kiss, before they disappeared into the woods.

I didn't mention the girl before because I was jealous, didn't want to discuss another girl with him, didn't want to know anything about her. But it just popped out of me, without warning, like a hiccup you don't expect.

Nothing has been the same since.

He changed. Because he knows I caught him in a lie.

Now we are in the van again and it's obvious that he doesn't want to be seen with me. He told me to sit in the back seat, which makes me claustrophobic because there are no back seat windows. He has also stopped talking to me.

Since he told me it was time to go as we were feeding the swans, he has hardly said anything. He has not looked at me, either. He is almost hunched over the steering wheel and he keeps glancing in the side-view mirror as if he is trying to spot someone following us.

A minute ago, I asked him where we were going and he didn't answer.

He is like two people in one body—the nice guy who bought me hot dogs and asked me about the scars on my wrists and the guy with cold eyes who is a stranger, like now at the steering wheel.

I am not only claustrophobic here in the back seat. I also feel trapped.

And I'm also scared.

He drove out of the park and on to the highway in a jumble of emotions, needing time to sort things out. He knew that he must eliminate the girl, cleverly, leaving no trail or clues behind. He must also get in touch with Maria Valdez, could feel the need growing in him, gnawing at him like a huge emptiness that must be filled as soon as possible.

Glancing in the side-view mirror, he saw only the normal flow of traffic behind him. He decided at last, finally, that he was not being followed and that he had not been followed since leaving Wickburg. All along, he had been alert to suspicious cars and had found none. There had been no police cruiser at the park, and it would have been impossible for any car, suspicious or otherwise, to drive into the park without being observed.

He looked into the back seat and saw the girl scrunched up, hugging herself like a little kid. Now that he had condemned her, he felt a rush of tenderness towards her, not the kind he'd found with the other girls or that he'd seek with Maria Valdez, but a different tenderness, want-ing to be gentle with her. Her face, moist with perspiration, was a bit puffy under her eyes, showing the effects of the heat or maybe simply weariness from sleeping all cramped up in the van last night. He'd allowed her to freshen up in the single rest-room at the pavilion, giving her two minutes to do the job, after checking to see if there was a rear entrance or a window through which she could escape. She'd been fresh-faced and eager, eyes bright, when she came out. But as he glanced at her again, he caught a look of apprehension—or was it fear?—in her eyes, a shadow falling across her face. Maybe she suspected what was going to happen to her.

He had to take away any fear she might have, that might make her do something desperate and call attention to them.

He pulled to the side of the highway. "Why don't you come into the front seat?" he said. "Sit beside me so we can talk."

"Why did you put me here in the first place?" she asked, still suspicious.

"Okay—I was afraid we were being followed, that the police might think I'd kidnapped you. You're just a kid, a runaway. I can't afford to get into trouble . . ."

Her face softened. She pushed a lock of hair from her forehead. Opened the door and scrambled into the front seat. "Thank you. I was getting claustrophobic back there." Touching his arm lightly, she said, "I'll be quiet."

"Just be yourself," he said. "And I'll try, too. Be patient with me. I've been locked up for three years. I get tense once in a while. I'm still trying to get back to normal." He bestowed upon her his best smile, not faking it, wanting her to trust him, to take away her doubts.

"Okay," she said, the brightness back in her eyes again, and he marvelled at the power he had to affect her, like pushing buttons to make her happy or sad. Or afraid.

He pushed another button, touching her hand where it rested on her knee.

"It's nice having you with me," he said. And found that the words came easy to him.

His touch is like those small shocks of electricity you get when you walk on a thick carpet.

He draws his hand quickly away but his touch remains like an after-burn on my skin.

His smile is dazzling but more than that. There's affection in it. Mr Sinclair once said that *affection* is one of the most neglected words in the English language, that people throw the word *love* around like confetti when they mean *affection*. And that affection is a special feeling that you can have for a person.

But I think affection is also sad, especially when a person wants more than affection, wants love and can't have it.

"Eric." I love saying his name.

"What?" he asks, absently as usual, as if he is thinking of other things and has not actually heard me.

"I think my fixation is gone."

"Good." He turns slightly towards me, a half-smile on his lips. Then back to the highway again.

"I think I'm falling in love with you instead."

He does not answer. The car shoots forward, picking up speed.

"That's not a smart thing to do," he says, finally, speaking slowly, as if he has rehearsed the words in his mind. "How do you know what love is, anyway? You're just a kid . . ."

I move my body but I feel cheap doing it because my body doesn't excite him. Or at least he pretends it doesn't.

"I'm almost sixteen," I reply. "And love's got nothing to do with age. Romeo and Juliet. Juliet was fourteen. I never felt this way before. Well, maybe a little." Thinking of Mr Sinclair.

"With who?" he asks, but as if he's humouring me, making conversation.

"A teacher, Mr Sinclair."

"Did he know you had this feeling for him?"

"Maybe, because he was afraid of me."

"Why was he afraid of you?"

"Afraid he might get into trouble if he touched me, showed me how he felt."

He doesn't reply but keeps his eyes on the highway, still glancing in the rear-view mirror once in a while.

We cruise along, the windows open, wind blowing my hair, talking once in a while, and even the silences are nice. I place my hand on his knee, and he allows it to remain there.

Turning off the highway, we drive through country roads, dappled with sunlight, gentle breezes coming into the car now and not stiff winds.

We drive into the centre of a town whose name I don't know and it doesn't matter. As we slowly pass a bus terminal, I feel him stiffen beside me, actually feel him going rigid, his knuckles on the steering wheel turning white. He swivels into a parking space and is staring out my side window.

I follow his gaze and see her. She is tall, with long black hair flowing down her back, almost to her waist. She's wearing a long brown paisley skirt and a white blouse. Her head is tilted as she looks in the window of a clothing store. The look in his eyes startles me, shocks me, in fact. Like glancing into his soul, something raw and naked there, such longing in his eyes but even more than longing. Like a hunger. I think of those horror movies I've seen, where a man turns into a werewolf in front of your eyes, camera tricks, changing from a regular person to an animal, hairy, with claws, glittering eyes. Eric doesn't turn into an animal, not hairy and no claws, but he has changed. The naked need in his eyes makes me shiver in the heat.

I take a deep breath.

"Why don't you go and speak to her?" I hear myself saying.

He glances at me as if he had forgotten I am here.

"She's beautiful," I say. "She's all by herself, alone. Maybe she's lonesome."

I hate myself for telling him this but I want him to be happy.

He shakes his head, more than once, twice, three times, as if he's trying to shake off not only my words but something inside of him.

"Go ahead," I urge. "Talk to her. It's like she's waiting for you."

While I'm talking to him, I'm playing a trick with my mind, knowing what he might do if he goes to the girl, but not allowing myself to acknowledge what he might do, as if my mind is splitting in two, half in the light and half in shadows. I know what that need in his eyes means, what he might have done to those other girls, but I also deny it at the same time: he's only a regular guy who's seen a good-looking girl on the street and wants to pick her up.

"I love you," I say. "I want you to be happy. Go to her."

He has one hand on the door handle and I think he is about to launch himself from the van when I say, "Wait."

As we both look at her, the girl turns away from the store window, eyes bright with anticipation as a guy with a briefcase arrives wearing a beige summer suit. She greets him

with a big smile as he bends to touch his lips briefly to her
cheek.

Eric guns the engine, his foot slamming the accelerator,
the smell of exhaust enveloping the van.

"Let's go," he says, his voice harsh and bitter.

And we go.

How much does she know? he wondered as they headed
towards the highway again, silence in the van, the girl
looking out of her window.

They hadn't spoken since they left the town behind. He
didn't know what to say to her. Afraid of what he *might* say.
She had urged him to pick up the girl. He'd heard the
urgency in her voice, like she was cheering him on. As if she
knew what he was going to do and didn't care. She said she
loved him—does love go that far?

Actually, he was relieved now that the guy with the
briefcase had come along, taking away any decision he might
have had to make. The situation had been filled with danger.
Broad daylight and a strange town. The girl in the van
practically a witness. Yet the need inside him had been so
intense that he might have capitulated, might have made a
disastrous error.

"I could use a shower," the girl said, breaking the silence
at last. "I feel all grimy . . ."

Her face was innocent of deceit as he glanced at her.

His thoughts raced ahead. Seized a solution, a course of
action. "We can stay at a motel tonight. You can shower all
you want." Then added, "Don't worry—twin beds. Then we
can find a nice restaurant." He thought grimly: *like a
prisoner's last meal.* Then, some time in the night, a quiet
goodbye. Maybe with a pillow, quick and silent.

"Know what I feel like having?" she said, all eagerness. "A real turkey dinner, just like Thanksgiving . . ."

"Too hot," he said. "I thought girls like salads, stuff like that . . ."

He was enjoying this stupid conversation about what to eat.

"That girl back there. She was so beautiful," she said. "Dressed nice. Did you notice her outfit? I'd love to have clothes like that some day . . ." Wistful, kind of sad.

"Why some day?" he asked. "Why not today?"

He felt reckless with generosity, knowing that he held this girl's life in his hands, had the power to make her happy or sad.

For the moment, why not make her happy?

"We'll find a good store in the next town," he said. "We'll go on a shopping spree."

Everything in the store was black and white, from the stripes on the walls to the swirl of tiles on the floor.

The woman who came forward from the back of the store was attired entirely in black, which drew Eric's eyes to the white streak in her hair.

"A dress," the girl told her, her voice wispy and small.

The woman sized up the girl with eyes as impersonal as an X-ray technician's. The girl glanced beseechingly at Eric: help me, her eyes pleaded.

Eric waved his hand extravagantly. "Get more than a dress," he said. "Some sporty things, blouses . . ."

"Tops," the clerk said, correcting him, taking him in at a glance, then dismissing him completely.

As the girl flicked through a rack of dresses, he was struck by the irony of the situation. She would never have the opportunity to wear the clothes to a dance or on a date. The purchases would be a waste of money, in fact. Yet he enjoyed the prospect of spending money on her.

The girl disappeared into a dressing-room, two or three dresses over her arm, glancing back at him with a delighted smile. The clerk went to the window and looked out, ignoring him, glancing at her watch occasionally.

The girl flounced out of the dressing-room, radiating bliss, the dress a dazzle of bright red-and-yellow flowers. Face flushed, eyes brilliant, she asked, "What do you think?"

He knew that it did not matter what he thought. It was obvious that she loved this garish dress she'd never wear.

"Beautiful," he said. It did not cost him anything to say it. He displayed his old smile, charm and shyness, that always worked.

She also bought other stuff—two or three tops, a short beige skirt—too short, he thought, amazed at how her taste ran counter to his.

He saw a big white hat on the head of a faceless mannequin, reminiscent of the hat that girl had worn in the canoe. He took it off the mannequin and brought it to the girl in both hands, like an offering.

"Oh, Eric," she cried happily.

While the clerk stood by, looking at floor or ceiling but never at them.

As Eric peeled off twenty-dollar bills to pay for the purchases, the clerk drew away in surprise. "Cash?" As if pronouncing a foreign word.

"Keep the change," Eric said, knowing how stupid that sounded despite the contempt in his voice.

The clerk, finally, raised her eyes to his.

Eric smiled at her, a smile of promise and menace, and saw her flinch. Let her take that to bed with her tonight, he thought, as he left the store with the girl.

Outside, she said, "I should have freshened up before going in there. I feel all icky . . ."

"You're fine," he said.

They bought a hair-drier in a drugstore in response to her remark that her hair would be a mess after a shower without a drier.

"Why not some perfume?" he suggested as they walked by a counter displaying pyramids of fancy boxes, some blue, some green, the scent of flowers in the air.

"I like the smell of soap," the girl said. "And anyway you should save your money."

She touched his arm, somehow an intimate gesture, as if they were a couple going steady, putting aside money for an engagement ring. Like so many stupid movies he'd seen.

At the motel she dumped the boxes and plastic bags on the twin bed she'd chosen and sighed, blowing air out of the corner of her mouth.

"Shower time," she announced. "Then I'll put on a fashion show for you . . ."

He stared at the blank television screen, waiting for her, listening to the sound of water jetting from the shower head, hearing her voice above it all—was she singing? He remembered sitting like this in the facility for hours at a time, trying to keep his mind as blank as the featureless tube before him. Then he filled the blank with Maria Valdez, dusky and dark, imagining what she would look like taking a shower, water streaming down her sleek body, her black hair clustered on her flesh.

"Don't look," the girl commanded, invading the room, filling the air with the clean, brisk smell of pine.

Listening to the rustle of clothing as she dressed, he was amazed at the series of events that had brought him here to this room, so different from what he imagined his first day of real freedom would be like.

"Okay," she said. "You can turn around now . . ."

She was wearing a dress she had not shown him at the store, white, shimmering with sequins, a sparkling senior prom kind of dress that reached her ankles. Her blonde hair sparkled, too, loose and full, cascading to her shoulders. She was barefoot, which made her seem too young for the dress, like a little girl trying on her mother's clothes. Except for the fullness of her breasts.

She twirled in front of him, imitating actresses she'd probably seen in movies, hair whirling, too, and her eyes as radiant as the sequins in the dress.

Stopping suddenly, she declared, "I love you, Eric. Not because you bought me all this stuff but because . . ."

He raised his finger to his lips.

"Shhh," he said.

Later, at a restaurant across from the motel, she confessed, "I knew that you didn't like that flowered dress. That's why I chose the white one."

He marvelled at how she had read his thoughts, had seen behind the expression on his face, unconvinced by the Eric Poole charm. Another reason to eliminate her.

For dessert she ordered chocolate cake topped with whipped cream but pushed it away half-eaten. Sagging with weariness, she said, "I'm pooped. It's been a long day . . ."

He agreed, signalling the waitress for the check.

153

"But it turned out to be a good day, didn't it, Eric?" Looking to him for confirmation.

"Yes," he said.

That was not the moment to speak the truth.

He lay in bed, waiting for her to go to sleep. He didn't have to wait long. Like a child, she'd curled up in the sheet, yawning, murmuring, "Night, Eric," then, hand tucked under her chin, she drifted off, small snoring sounds coming from her after a while.

He snapped off the lamp beside his bed and let his eyes become accustomed to the darkness. The events of the day caught up with him, images flashing in his mind. The van, the highway, the park, and, most of all, the girl entering his life, changing his plans, forcing him to do the unexpected. Yet he was grateful to her, in a way. She had introduced him to the world of people, preparing him for social situations, conversations, sauntering in a park. He was glad that he had bought the new clothes, insisted on the chocolate cake for dessert. Little enough to pay her back.

The girl stirred and he squinted at her through the half darkness. Bands of light sifting through the venetian blinds laddered her body. Her snores were deep, vibrating. The snoring stopped and she murmured in her sleep, words he could not understand. The digital clock read 1:07. Which surprised him. He must have dozed off without being aware of it.

He reviewed his plan, assessing the risks. There were

always risks, of course, and he had learned to accept them as his way of life. The biggest risk would be carrying her body to the van, although he had tried to minimize it. He had insisted on a room at the far end of the motel. Had backed the van up to the door of the room. He'd left the van unlocked for easy entry. It would take less than a minute to carry her body the few feet to the van and place her inside. Earlier tonight, he had loosened the outside bulb in the lighting fixture next to the door. He would dispose of the body later in the usual way.

Finally, he sat up in bed and groped for the pillow. His bare feet touched the floor, the carpet soft, his movements noiseless. He then stood still, counting slowly to fifty, listening to the rhythm of her breathing. She had thrown off her sheet. Her T-shirt had bunched up above her stomach, revealing flesh as pale as the moon, the indentation of her navel. He moved, his shadow falling across her body, obliterating her momentarily.

He held the pillow in front of him like a shield. He had done his mother this way. Seemed like the kindest way to do it—you did not see the face during the struggle. And the struggle was feeble and brief.

Next to the bed now, hovering over her, he gathered himself, his legs spread apart to provide leverage, her body bathed in pale light.

As he raised the pillow, her eyes flew open and she looked directly up at him.

Then: her eyes wide with fear, her mouth open as if she was silently screaming.

They stared at each other—he didn't know how long.

Her face suddenly softened.

"Don't you know I love you?" she said, as if that would stop him, could solve everything.

Closing her eyes, she sighed. "Go ahead, then. Do it."

He lowered the pillow, stood uncertainly beside her bed. Outside, a car ghosted past the motel, its sound dying in the distance.

He let the pillow drop to the floor.

Half sitting up, leaning on one elbow, she looked up at him.

"Were you really going to do it?" she asked.

"Yes," he said.

But in my heart, where it counts the most, I know he wouldn't have done it. For a moment, yes, I was terrified, without even seeing the pillow, only saw his face, pale and cold, like the face on a coin. But the pillow brought the terror, and I wonder now if I screamed. I don't think so, because he just stood there and dropped the pillow, and now I know that I'm safe. If he didn't do it here in a quiet motel away from everybody, when would he do it? Never, I tell myself while he's still standing there, looking down at me.

I want to hear his voice, want to hear him talk.

"You didn't do it," I say. "Because you couldn't."

He still doesn't say anything.

"Could you?"

The calmness of my voice surprises me because I am shaking inside, my stomach churning and my heart clumping against my ribs.

A frown scrawls itself across his forehead, like scribbles on white paper.

"No," he says, finally. "I couldn't."

"That's because I love you, and you know it. I'm not like the other girls . . ." Thinking of that girl near the railroad tracks and the girls that the reporter had mentioned.

His frown deepens and I wonder if I've gone too far, but I figure I have nothing to lose. And I can't seem to stop talking, as if my fear has given me a shot of energy. The fear is gone but my blood is sizzling in my veins, like needle points stinging me from the inside.

"I will love you for ever, Eric. And I'll never betray you . . ."

"Don't," he says, waving my words away, his hand like a pale bird in the half darkness. Then he makes his way back to bed, sliding in, pulling the sheet over his shoulders, facing away from me.

I lie awake, listening to my heartbeats, slower now, and I replay in my mind the words I had spoken, wondering how much was true—did I really love him?—or had I been talking crazy because I was so mixed up, scared and exhilarated at the same time.

What you should do is get out of here, wait for him to fall asleep, then slip away, as far as you can go.

But I think of that shopping spree, and the dress he bought me, and how he even wanted to buy me perfume. Plus chocolate cake for dessert.

My mind and body begin to drift on the soft cloud the mattress has become and I am so tired, such a sweet tiredness that softens all my bones, and I give myself up to the oblivion of sleep and whatever will happen in that oblivion.

They sat in the motel restaurant waiting for breakfast to be served. Not really a restaurant but a coffee shop, breakfast consisting merely of coffee and either doughnuts, bagels, or Danish pastry.

The legs of the small table at which he and the girl sat were uneven, and the table rocked unsteadily as he leaned his elbows on it. He felt the girl's eyes on him and looked away but there was nothing much to see. A couple of truck drivers hunched over their coffee, a waitress scurrying from table to table, middle-aged, harassed, soiled apron limp against her thighs.

The girl's eyes disturbed him, looking at him imploringly, full of the thing he did not want to see in them. He had expected her to regard him fearfully this morning. Instead, this tender gaze. He looked away again, at the street, where heat haze had gathered already, like steam from a boiling kettle.

He was waiting for the girl to say something, but did not want to hear it. She had barely spoken this morning, only a murmured *hello* as she dressed, careless with her body as usual, displaying a flash of thigh, the swing of her breasts.

He had dressed hurriedly, then went into the bathroom, seeing, in his peripheral vision, her eyes upon him. He killed time shaving, deliberately passing the razor over his face until his skin became sensitive to the touch. When he emerged from the bathroom, she was standing at the doorway, one hand on the knob.

Now in the coffee shop, waiting for their orders, she said, "Would you look at me, please? You make me feel like I'm not here."

He rested his eyes upon her.

"That's better," she said, as their food arrived: orange juice and a jelly doughnut for her, coffee with cream and sugar for him, still trying to adjust to ex-facility coffee.

"I love you," she said matter-of-factly, as if commenting on the heat of the morning, taking a huge bite of the doughnut, the jelly oozing over her fingers.

"Please don't say that," he said.

He really wanted to say: *I almost killed you last night, don't you realize that? I still might do it.*

"Why didn't you run away after I fell asleep?" he asked. "You could have gotten away. Could have taken money out of my wallet . . ."

"I thought of that," she admitted. "But I wanted to stay with you. You're the only person who's ever treated me with respect. And I trust you . . ."

He sipped his coffee, marvelling at her innocence, her willingness to trust him, after all that had happened. But what had happened? Nothing really. As he watched her tongue licking jelly from her cheek, he wondered what it would be like to kiss the jelly off that cheek, to feel her body close to him, not like with the others, but stopping before the act was completed. Maybe there would be tenderness in all that. His thoughts startled him: *What's happening here? Why am I thinking this way?*

160

"Give me a chance," she said. "I'll only speak when spoken to. I won't bug you with questions." A small smile appeared on her face, a touch of mischief in it: "Who knows? I may steal into your heart a little bit." Then serious again: "I don't expect you to love me back. But be tender." Taking another bite of the doughnut. "I'm still a virgin, technically . . ."

Despite himself, not wanting further conversation with her, not wanting to discuss her virginity, of all things, he asked, "What do you mean, technically?"

"I mean, I've never slept with anybody. Never had intercourse. But I've been touched. And kissed. Everywhere. Well, not everywhere . . ."

His cheeks growing warm, he wondered at her ability to constantly surprise him, keeping him on edge, off balance. And now an unexpected excitement attached to the surprise. She'd said: *Be tender.*

"I don't want to talk about that stuff," he said lamely.

The waitress interrupted, pouring more coffee into his cup before he had asked. "A bottomless cup," she said, spilling some on the table.

"I hope I'm not embarrassing you," the girl said, chewing the last of the doughnut.

He had an impulse to say: *Don't speak with your mouth full of food,* the way you'd talk to a child, the way his mother talked to him when he was just a little kid. An order softened by affection. Before she met Harvey. He had not thought about those tender moments for a long time, the moments he and his mother shared, curled up in bed together as she read him a bedtime story, and afterwards her hair tumbling against his cheek, her perfume invading his pores, becoming a part of him.

"Everything okay?"

161

He didn't answer, heard her voice from far away, thinking of his mother, her presence almost palpable, as if overnight, in a dream he couldn't remember, a door had been opened and she'd stepped across a dim threshold. He remembered dark nights, her long black hair enveloping him, her lips trailing across his flesh . . . *my darling, Eric . . . my darling . . .*

"Eric . . ."

The girl's voice reached him from far distances.

"Yes."

"Remember what I said last night?"

"What did you say?" he asked, bringing himself back to the present: the coffee shop, here, now.

His mother had disappeared from his thoughts, like a wisp of smoke in a gust of wind.

"You know . . ."

She mouthed the words silently: *I'll never betray you.*

He realized she knew all about him but she didn't care.

"Let's go," he said, leaving the second cup of coffee untouched.

In the van, windows open, a sudden shifting of the winds freshening the air, he drove aimlessly through back roads, avoiding the major highways and cities.

The girl seemed content riding beside him. She had showered after breakfast, putting on one of the new tops, bright green, matching her eyes. Her new denim shorts were longer than her earlier pair, reaching to mid-thigh.

He enjoyed the countryside, pastures and meadowlands, slowed to watch cows grazing in a long field. Passing through small towns, he was pleased to see the white church steeples, town commons, to see the old Civil War monuments and cannons.

He and the girl did not say much, commented briefly on the passing scenery, yet he thought that they were communicating somehow. *I'll never betray you.*

Passing a pay telephone on a street corner, he thought again of Maria Valdez, the longing to see her, everything her body promised.

"I have to make a call," he said.

"Is it a girl?"

"Is what a girl?"

A look of annoyance, impatience on her face.

"Yes," he said. "It's a girl . . ."

"Then call her. See her. Don't let me stop you." Her face brightened and her voice grew light and playful. "I don't mind sharing you. I'll try not to be jealous. All right—I'll be jealous a little bit . . ."

"Stop it," he said, not in the mood for idle bantering. This was not a joking matter. If he saw Maria Valdez, his Señorita, the consequences would be nothing to joke about. And this girl would be a part of it all.

Glancing at her, he saw that her face had darkened, her eyes dropping away. "I'm sorry," she said. "It's just that I want you to do whatever you want. I saw a bus terminal at that last town. Why don't you just stop the car and let me off?"

"It's a van, not a car," he said.

"Whatever, just let me go. Forget about me and I'll forget about you. I mean, I'll make myself forget about you. And you don't have to worry. Nothing happened, right? You haven't done anything. You gave me a ride. You treated me very nice. You bought me some clothes. You didn't even touch me, which is more than I can say for other people. So, let me out, let me go . . ."

"No."

"Why not?"

"Because . . ."

A lot of reasons.

He felt safer with her at his side. If he left her behind now, he wouldn't know where she'd go or what she'd do. She was a loose cannon, with the power to explode at any moment. A link between him and Alicia Hunt. Glancing at her again, he saw that the new top was looser than yesterday's blouse and did not thrust her breasts at him. Her legs were tucked under her body. Good. Enough distractions without her body playing tricks.

"Because why?"

When he didn't answer, she said, "I saw a phone booth a while ago. Go back. Call her . . ."

Eric drove on, would find his own telephone in due time, allowing all the possibilities of Maria Valdez to fill his mind and body.

Maria Valdez answered immediately, her voice breathless in his ear, as if she'd been standing by the phone waiting for his call. "Hello." Music blared in the background, a child crying, or yelling, he wasn't sure which. Her child? The possibility stunned him. He could not picture his Señorita holding a child at her hip.

"Just a minute," she said, the words softened by her accent, the *t* in *minute* barely enunciated. The smell of gasoline filled his nostrils: the pay phone was next to a service station.

Back on the line, she said, "I'm baby-sittin'. My sister's baby while she's getting her hair done . . ." Paused, then hesitantly: "This you?"

164

"It's me," he said, pulse quickening.

"Where are you? I been waitin' for you to call."

"I got delayed. But I'm only a few miles away now. A place called Piper's Crossing."

"That's not far. Will I see you today? Tonight?"

Her eagerness inflamed him. He averted his face so that the girl in the nearby van could not see his expression.

"You still there?"

"Yes, I'm here." Then taking the plunge, glancing back at the van, seeing the girl's face, smiling, nodding, as if urging him on. "Today, tonight, whenever you say." He knew he was talking too fast, sounding too eager, but her voice excited him, racing through him. He pressed his thighs together, disguising what was happening to him.

"Later today. In the evening," she said.

Perfect, because he preferred the evening, which could turn to night-time, for whatever would happen.

"There's a carnival in town, at a place called Prospect Park," she said, in that low throwaway voice of hers. "It has a merry-go-round, makes me feel like a little girl again. I'll bring a picnic. We can go on the merry-go-round and then a picnic after. In the woods, I know a private place for us to be together . . ."

In her voice and the words she spoke, he heard the answer to all his desires and longings, the need for tenderness that he'd suppressed during all the long dry months at the facility, and the night-time visions that never measured up to the reality.

The child cried distantly in the background, and Maria Valdez shushed it.

"Where do I pick you up?" he asked.

"Better I meet you there," she said. "My family, they

watch me close, don't want me to get in trouble again so soon. My mother is like an old watchdog."

She gave him directions to Prospect Park. Simple: within sight of Route 21, the major highway between Piper's Crossing and Barton, Exit 25.

"My girlfriend, Anita, she'll drop me off if you'll bring me back." And then, almost formal, as if she had rehearsed the words, planning for their meeting: "It will be so good to see you up close, Eric Poole."

He closed his eyes, thinking of her long black hair, the white throat, the slender body, dusky skin. And the tenderness.

When he slipped into the van, the girl greeted him with a wide smile: "I see you scored . . ."

He did not answer, distracted, still in the thrall of Maria Valdez's voice, the imminence of their meeting and all the possibilities.

"What time? When?" the girl asked.

At last he answered, "Later today." Hearing the tremor in his voice.

I am always timid at carnivals. Went once with my mother and Dexter, who wanted to show off how big and brave he was, sitting in the front seat of the roller-coaster without holding on, waving both hands above his head as the car plunged down the steepest slope, and I wished, feeling guilty, that he would tumble out and land flat on the ground at our feet. Later, he kept hitting his fist in the palm of his hand, angry because that particular carnival did not have one of those attractions where he could slam down a mallet, hoping to make the bell ring so that he could brag about how strong he was.

He kept urging me to go on rides with him but I resisted. The rides were too scary. He promised to buy me all the ice-cream and soda pop I wanted or anything else, but I shook my head no. Then we came to the Ferris wheel and I finally agreed to go, but all alone. I did not want him sitting beside me, *near* me. I discovered that I loved that Ferris wheel, the way you rose up and reached the top, higher than the trees and surrounding buildings: next stop, the sky. Rocking the chair at the top when the wheel stopped, the music dim and distant, and not scared at all, but feeling how an angel must feel looking down at the world.

That's why I drift towards the Ferris wheel after watching

Eric go off with Maria Valdez. He finally told me her name only a few minutes ago as we drove up to the carnival. We spent a nice day driving around, stopping once in a while to look at the scenery, ate Big Macs at McDonald's, not saying much. We went by a lake in the afternoon, watched people swimming or sunning themselves on the beach, boats gliding on the water. I asked him about the prison, and he said it was not a prison but a facility for young people and also said he didn't want to talk about it. He asked me about my life and I made up a life for him about school and what kind of music and books I liked but not about my fixations or Gary or other stuff that happened to me. I told him my mother was a hair stylist and my father a fire-fighter who died rescuing children in a fire, all lies but not really, dreams made real for a few minutes by speaking them aloud.

Just before we drove up to the carnival, he said, "Someday, Lori, I want you to tell me the truth."

As he left the van to meet Maria Valdez, I saw the excitement in his eyes, more than excitement, that strange heat and longing that made him a sudden stranger to me.

She wore a white top, satin, bright as vanilla ice-cream, and her long black hair sparkled with sequins. Black hip-huggers clung to her long legs. A pretty face, too, dusky skin and a touch of lipstick like a smear of fire from a distance. I wish I could look like her, sleek and thin instead of this top of mine swishing around most of the time.

This top of mine is proving irresistible to the young guy operating the Ferris wheel. He is looking me up and down, but mostly up. He is only a kid but has a drooping moustache and a wispy beard.

"Hiya, babe," he says, as I hand him a five-dollar bill. *Babe*, of all things.

"Your money's no good here, babe," he says. "Not for something like you . . ."

"Take it," I say with my best don't-screw-around voice.

Funny thing. I always take for granted that males, young and old, look me up and down and if I smile they offer me all kinds of stuff for very little reason. Old Mr Stuyvesant would drink his wine and proclaim: *I would give you half my kingdom* as he did things, and I believed that he would if he had a kingdom. I also feel as if I hold some kind of power over men and boys, like this guy now at the Ferris wheel. So I surprise myself when I insist on paying, because I could save two dollars. You have to think of your future.

He reluctantly takes the five-dollar bill and slaps three dollars change in my palm.

With a scowl, he drops the chain and allows me to enter. I step into the chair and almost lose my balance as it sways with the sudden weight of my body. Sitting down, I buckle the safety strap around my waist.

"Have a great trip," the young guy calls, his voice loaded with sarcasm.

A guy and a girl sit in the chair ahead of me, clinging to each other, the girl squealing like she's supposed to, I guess, as the attendant slams back the control rod and off we go with a lurch, and a crazy kind of tinny Ferris wheel music begins to play. I take a deep breath and give myself over to the sensation of leaving the earth, a bit dizzy but a pleasant dizziness as the trees and buildings recede and the sky spreads out before me when I raise my eyes. I am rocking in the chair like a baby in a cradle. As I sweep to the top, I look down at the tilted landscape and see Eric and Maria Valdez walking side by side, holding hands, heading for the picnic grove. A picnic basket swings from her other hand. Jealousy streaks through me as I remember our own picnic grove, where the swans drifted in the water. Then tell myself, *What do you mean, your own picnic grove? It was never yours or his— just a spot you stopped at to get off the road and a bite to eat.* But I remember that girl in the canoe with her big white hat and her arm trailing in the water. I swoop down and up again and the young couple still cling to each other, but they get off at the next stop, the girl dizzy, holding on to the guy for support, and he grins and looks pleased as he guides her into the crowd.

Other people get on now, children with parents, and another couple and a guy all by himself eating popcorn, and we rise again and I sit back, a kind of letting go, and even letting Eric go out of my thoughts, not wanting to think about him in the woods with Maria Valdez, and what will happen and telling myself nothing will happen, nothing bad that is, and they will kiss each other, and touch and caress, and I don't want to go any further in my thoughts and instead rock the chair and give myself up to the moment, the music soft then loud as we go up and down and lights beginning to come on, twilight softening the entire world. I glance towards the picnic grove, and Eric and Maria Valdez are not there but why should they be there? I know that neither of them was really interested in food, and I picture them in the woods with the darkness coming on and tell myself, *Please don't think about it.*

The Ferris wheel comes to a halt with a lurch and I am at the absolute top, the chair swaying from the sudden stop. The kids in the other chairs are laughing and pointing around and I am above them, above everything else. I look down at the people strolling below. A blue balloon breaks free, slipping from a child's hand, coming up, passing by almost as if I could reach out and grab it—wouldn't that be nice, rescuing a balloon for a child crying down below?

I look towards the street and spot a brown van parked near the entrance. The van sparks a dim memory I can't pin down. A man stands outside the van with a portable telephone at his ear. I have seen that van before. I have seen it, but where? The knowledge explodes in my mind. On the street next to Eric's aunt's house, the van that the reporter back in Wickburg had pointed out to me, a surveillance van. *They're keeping tabs on him.* I see clearly now what is happening. They have set a trap for Eric.

"Let me down," I call to the operator, leaning precariously out of the chair as it swings, but my voice is lost in all the noise.

I yell louder and louder, but my voice doesn't carry over the crazy tinny music and the happy cries and laughter of the children. The guy with the popcorn two chairs below sees me and laughs, probably thinking that the height has panicked me, and he is very amused. I call down again and this time my voice is loud, in a sudden silence between the ending of the song and the beginning of a new one.

"Let me down. It's important. Please."

I hear my voice and the urgency in it and so does the operator, but he looks up and smiles as if he's enjoying my predicament.

Four men are emerging from the van. They are dressed in ordinary work clothes but I am sure they are cops. One of them is an old man, a cigarette dangling from his lips as he hurries to keep up with the others.

"Please," I cry desperately, looking down again, and the operator frowns, uncertain now. The children begin yelling and I stand up, losing my balance, struggle to regain it.

"Don't do anything crazy," the guy with the popcorn yells.

A hush falls over the Ferris wheel as if everyone has taken a deep breath. I cling to one of the wires supporting the chair. In the silence, the voice of the popcorn guy breaks through:

"Let her down, for Christ's sake."

Bowing his head, the operator starts the Ferris wheel moving again. I see the men from the van entering the park.

Eric and the Señorita stood in a clearing in the woods, away from the heat and the tumult of the carnival, the Señorita's hand in his hand, her hip brushing his hip. He'd offered to carry the picnic basket but she'd demurred. "A woman carries the food," she said, a throwback, he supposed, to her upbringing. Which pleased him: a girl, a woman, who knew her place in the world.

She asked, "Why is your hand so cold . . . ?"

Eric was caught by surprise, not aware that his hand was either hot or cold, dry or sweating.

"Well, not cold exactly but not warm, either," she amended, smiling, the white teeth contrasted with the dusky skin, her black hair swirling, her voice intimate.

No apology necessary, he thought, smiling back at her, the shy wistful smile, sweetness pumping through his body like the first taste of chocolate when he was a little kid. Seeing her up close now, he realized that she was older than she'd looked from across the cafeteria at the facility, and her make-up heavy.

"This is a nice quiet place," she said, looking around. Grass at their feet, thick bushes and undergrowth surrounding the spot.

"No picnic table, but we can eat later," she said, placing the basket on the grass and stretching her arms, reaching up to the sky but looking at him with those dark eyes.

The carnival music dim in the distance, the spot where they stood was hushed in silence, shadowed by tall trees.

He looked at her, tenderness in his glance, and the excitement began to grow inside him. He had waited so long for this moment, the Señorita and himself alone at last, his heart beginning to accelerate and juices gathering in his mouth, making it difficult for him to swallow. She dropped to the ground, gracefully, like a flower petal, head resting against the picnic basket, her face raised to his, a hint of pink tongue between her lips.

His fingers twitched beyond his control. He went towards her, discarding all thought, all risks, all caution, plunging into the intimacy of the moment and all it promised.

"Eric!"

He heard his name like an echo in his brain, distant, a small irritation he shook off, not wanting to spoil this moment. He bent to the Señorita, open for him now, arms and face upraised.

"Eric!"

Again that voice, the intrusion, no longer distant as if from a dream but closer now, urgent, fracturing the intimacy. He heard the crackle of tree branches and the rustle of bushes being pushed aside. Then:

"Don't!"

The word like a blunt instrument striking him, causing him to halt, as if caught in mid-air.

Instantly he stilled, went from heat to cold, heart stopped, legs rigid.

173

"Don't touch her."

The girl's voice was close by now, and in a moment she burst out of the woods into clear view, hair wild, gasping:

"It's a trap, Eric. The cops ... they're here ... everywhere ..."

A moan escaped from him, and he looked down to see Maria Valdez grabbing the picnic basket, holding it in front of her like a shield as she scuttled away, lips tight and thin over her teeth, no longer the Señorita, all allure gone, all attraction vanished.

Before he could move and get out of this place, old Lieutenant Proctor, pushing aside branches, breathing heavily, stepped into the clearing, followed by three men who were obviously cops. One cop spoke with hushed voice into a portable telephone. The old lieutenant regarded Eric balefully, lips curled in distaste.

Eric's blood pulsed in his temples, his cheeks flooding with warmth. *She betrayed me.* He looked around wildly, felt trapped. Had never been trapped before. Had always been in control. Facing the lieutenant now, he tried to fix the old smile on his face, The Charm, but his lips were stiff, like plastic. He tried to wet his lips with his tongue but his mouth was dry.

"Still the monster, aren't you, Eric?" the old cop said, his voice heavy with contempt.

Eric swallowed hard, had to say something, had to gain control.

"Sticks and stones," he finally replied, relieved that he could speak, could find words to answer the old cop. "Names mean nothing to me, Lieutenant." But wanted to say, *I'm not a monster.* Monsters come out of the woods at night, lurk in cemeteries, prowl the dark for victims. I'm Eric Poole. *My, isn't he a sweet little boy, Mrs Poole?*

"He didn't do anything," the girl said, stepping towards the old cop defiantly, still out of breath, hair dishevelled, but defiant.

The lieutenant directed his attention at her. "Obstructing justice, miss," he said. "You could be in a lot of trouble. Under-age and a runaway."

"She didn't do anything, either," Eric offered, confidence returning as the girl looked gratefully at him.

Ignoring him, the old cop told her, "We can turn you over to the DYS, they deal with kids. For your own protection." Nodding to Eric, meaning: protection from him. His voice more kindly, he said, "Or we can arrange to have you go home. Where you belong . . ."

Without warning, the girl bolted, moving suddenly, as if fired from a rocket, crashing recklessly through the bushes, falling to one knee, regaining balance, bounding out of sight.

"Get her," the lieutenant snapped, and two of the cops set out in pursuit.

The lieutenant turned away from Eric, lit a cigarette, holding the match with cupped fingers. The carnival music grew loud in the gathering dusk, as if someone had turned up the volume.

"I'm free to go, right, Lieutenant?" Eric said, unable to hide the taunting in his voice.

"You can go, Eric. But you're not free. You'll never be free . . ."

Shaking his head, Eric said, "You never give up, do you? You've got me all wrong. I haven't touched that girl. I've been taking care of her. I'm going to take her home . . ."

The two cops returned, flushed and out of breath. "Couldn't find her anywhere, Lieutenant," the telephone cop said. "She could be hiding in a thousand places in these woods . . ."

"Better see that she stays safe, Eric," the old cop warned. "Anything happens to her and that's the end. Even if her body doesn't turn up."

"Nothing's going to happen to her," Eric said.

The old lieutenant looked older than ever now, if that was possible, his face like a death mask Eric had seen once in a horror movie.

He surprised himself by almost feeling sorry for the old cop, then remembered what the lieutenant had called him.

I'm not that, Eric thought.

Turning away, he said nothing, not even goodbye.

PART IV

The big white hat was perched precariously on her head, and she held it in place with her hand as the wind gusted, rocking the canoe a bit, the waves lapping at the edges. She exulted in the tossing of the wind, the movement of the canoe, the rippling waves, smiling, giggling at times.

"Isn't this beautiful?" she said. Like a little girl at a party.

Eric smiled, enjoying the sight of her. He was still in the glow of his escape from Lieutenant Proctor and his team of cops, recalling the frustration and disappointment on the old cop's face, and the dismay and disgust of the others, the resentment in their eyes as they turned away from him. Eric's triumph, of course, was tainted—the glorious moment with the traitor he'd called the Señorita spoiled and gone for ever.

The girl had finally turned up hours later as he sat waiting in the van. He knew she'd show up eventually, figured that she'd hidden in the woods until the coast was clear. Long after the carnival had ceased operating, the lingering crowds dispersed, the amusement rides still and silent, she had crept out of the woods, weary and rumpled, face smudged, hair limp and moist. "I'm a mess," she declared, crawling into the van.

179

"Thank you," Eric said, the words almost sticking in his throat. He had never spoken those particular words to anyone in a meaningful way. No one had ever done anything to deserve them. "You were—fine," he said, the compliment startling him even as he spoke. Yet he knew the truth of the word. Without the girl's intervention, he would have been caught in the act, under arrest somewhere, not in a youth facility this time but in a prison.

They had not gone to a motel last night but found a deserted area off the highway, near a meandering brook. The girl spent the night in the sleeping bag while he lay a short distance away, wrapping himself in a blanket as the night air grew cold. He didn't really sleep, the ground hard beneath him, his senses alert, his body tense. He listened to the night sounds, the occasional throb of a car from the highway, small scurryings in the woods, the noise of insects that he couldn't identify.

A new sound reached him, and he looked up to see the girl approaching, dragging the sleeping bag behind her.

"What's the matter?" he asked.

"I'm scared," she whispered. "I thought this would be fun, but it's spooky out here."

She was beautiful in the moonlight, her hair silver, her face like a pale cameo his mother had worn Sundays. But she was not dark like Maria Valdez and the others. She evoked gentleness in him, a desire to protect her even from the noises of the night. He wondered, *Is there something wrong with me?*

"Sleep next to me," he said.

She slipped into the sleeping bag and he curled up beside her and heard her soft sleeping noises after a while.

Early this afternoon she had spotted a sign proclaiming

MIRROR LAKE—SWIMMING, BOATING, PICNIC TABLES. A FAMILY PLACE.

"Let's stop," she said. "Please, please . . ."

He did not resist her pleas. He needed a place to pause, to make his plans. And he owed her a few minutes of pleasure.

She frolicked on the beach, dashing into the water now and then, having rolled her shorts impossibly high on her thighs. After a while a young girl joined her, splashing her legs and running away, then coming back again. She was like a child herself, chasing the little girl, whooping, while the girl's family smiled their approval. Other families were spread out on blankets.

He watched the girl absently, his thoughts moving towards the future. The future as near as tomorrow. He had to plan his next move. He knew that Lieutenant Proctor was smarter and more subtle than he had given him credit for, and wondered whether the old cop had more tricks up his sleeve, more traps to be sprung.

He had to start again. Get rid of the van. Send the girl home. Had to get out of New England and go as far away as possible. Grow a beard, shave his head—do something to disguise himself.

The girl stood before him, gesturing towards the lake where an old man and a child passed by in a canoe.

"Take me for a canoe ride," she said.

"No, it's getting late. You can't swim."

"They rent out life jackets along with the canoe. Please, Eric. Why did you buy me that hat if you didn't want to take me out on the water?"

"I didn't buy you a canoe—I bought you a hat."

Thinking that sounded clever. Surprised he'd suddenly made a kind of joke.

"It'll be romantic," she said. "Like the movies . . ."

They rented a canoe and a life jacket for her. He had been instructed in canoeing during a week at summer camp when he was twelve or thirteen and had no trouble remembering the routine. The girl settled down at the far end in her white hat, her hand trailing in the water, like the girl they'd watched two days ago.

The afternoon turned into evening, as they cruised the lake, near the shore at first. Then venturing further out. The effort of paddling reminded him that he had not exercised at all since leaving the facility. He had to get in shape again, begin a routine of working out, jogging. His arm muscles ached. He rested, letting the canoe drift. The girl stared dreamily at the water.

I love the breeze on my face, the smell of the air and the water, never realized that water actually has a smell to it, clean and fresh, and Eric is handsome as he paddles the canoe, shifting the paddle from one side to another, and I half-close my eyes, squinting at him, and he looks at me with an expression on his face that I can't really pin down—I search for a word and come up with an old-fashioned one that nobody uses any more but you read it in stories. *Fondly.* He looks at me fondly. I know that the look doesn't have love in it. Or even lust. I still wonder about love or sex or lust. I saw lust in his eyes when he looked at that girl on the sidewalk. That same lust when he spoke about Maria Valdez. I love him, anyway. I love him because he's kind to me and he doesn't want my body, doesn't want to feel me or touch me, like all the others—old Mr Stuyvesant and the guy at Aud-Vid Land and Dexter and even Gary—and maybe after a while he might look at me with more than fondness, will kiss me sweetly, tenderly.

I feel so free here in the canoe. I want to shout it to the world. I want to get rid of this life jacket, too tight across my top, digging into my shoulder blades, want to stand up and yell, *Look at me. I'm Lori Cranston . . .*

As he gazed absently at the girl, thinking how little it took to make her happy—a few new clothes at a store, a canoe ride—she began to take off her life jacket.

"What are you doing?" he asked, amazed again at her capacity to catch him by surprise.

"It's too tight," she said. "I want to feel free." Slipping out of the jacket, letting it drop to the floor of the canoe. "There, that's better . . ." Stretching, luxuriating, raising her face to the sky, the white hat perched precariously on her head.

She got to her feet, flinging her arms outwards, calling to the wind, the sky, the water. "I'm Lori Cranston, queen of the sea. The happiest girl in the world . . ."

The canoe rocked dangerously beneath them.

"Sit down," he ordered, alarm in his voice. "Please sit down." As she was about to reply, she lost her balance, her arms flailing the air, her hat taken by the wind and flung away like a huge white bird that had forgotten how to fly. As she swivelled around, trying to regain control, she was swooped away as if by invisible hands and plopped into the water, arms grappling at air, panic flashing in her eyes, as she disappeared from view. The canoe wobbled, almost overturned.

Instinctively, without thought, he dived into the water,

shocked by the sudden cold, knifing below the surface, trying to focus, saw her struggling frantically. He reached for her but she began to sink, as if in slow motion, her mouth agape, eyes wild with fright. He dipped, grabbed at her, clutched her fiercely. She kicked against him, then grabbed at him, her hands finding his shoulders, then his throat. He felt himself strangling, fought to break loose but needing to keep her in his grasp. She held on, frenzied, and they both sank lower. Needing air, he pushed for the surface, and she suddenly lost all resistance, ceasing to struggle, rising, rising with him.

They broke through the surface, and he gasped for breath, sweet air rushing into his lungs. She coughed, spluttered, eyes wild, still clutching him. He reached for the canoe for support, found it had overturned, flung one arm around it, holding the girl with the other . . .

God, I was drowning, Eric, terrified, dying, you saved me . . . I love you . . . love me, Eric . . .

. . . while she looked at him, eyes wild but gratitude in them, coughing, spluttering, huge coughs, eyes rolling back, writhing in his grasp. But the panic began again. Thrashing in his arms, she struck her head on the side of the canoe, the *thuck* of the collision loud in the silence of the lake. Suddenly she slipped out of his arms, and he saw, to his horror, that she had disappeared below the surface. He plunged into the water again, found her immediately, but she dragged him down with her, her arms around his neck, strangling as before in her panic. He struggled to free himself, knowing he needed air, needed to surface, or they would both sink to the bottom and drown. He managed to break loose, wrenching one arm away from her, wondering if he had broken it.

Arrowed to the surface, lungs burning, gasped for air, arms heavy with weariness. Dived again, searching—where was she?—nowhere to be seen ... up again, drawing deep breaths, canoe drifting away ... down again, must find her, must not give up ...

Later, darkness descending, he lay on the upended canoe, face down, paddling wearily with his arms, making slow progress towards shore as the sun went down, cheek pressed against the unyielding surface of the canoe. Paddle, rest a while, paddle. Not wanting to think of the girl, poor kid, somewhere below the water, cold and lost and alone. The lake was calm now, smooth and shiny like the lid of a coffin.

As he approached the shore, limp with exhaustion, he saw a gathering on the beach, huddled figures revealed in the whirling blue-red lights of police cruisers.

He moaned, the sound like a note of doom, as he continued paddling towards shore, knowing what was waiting for him there.

The old cop was standing at the stove waiting for the water to boil for tea when the telephone rang. He took his time going to the living-room and lifted the receiver without expectations.

"Hello," he said, clearing his throat. His cold was long gone and he blamed age for making his throat hoarse whenever he spoke after hours of silence.

"Great news, Lou," Pickett said, the brightness of his voice a contrast to recent morning calls in the aftermath of the failed trap for Eric Poole. "They've booked Eric Poole out in Springfield. First-degree murder."

The old cop's heart fluttered like a moth in his chest.

"That girl, the runaway. He killed her at a lake there. Took her out in a canoe. Claimed she panicked and fell overboard. But when her body was recovered, they found head trauma. From a blunt instrument. Maybe the paddle, which they haven't recovered yet."

The lieutenant sighed wearily, heard the whistle of the kettle as the water boiled.

"You there, Lou?" Pickett asked anxiously. "You okay?"

"I'm okay," he replied. "But Eric Poole was telling the truth, Jimmy. It *was* an accident. The girl wasn't his type. That wasn't his method of operation . . ."

Long pause, Pickett's disappointment palpable in his silence. The kettle continued to whistle.

"But it's all over, right, Lou?" Pickett asked.

The old cop thought of that child in the white First Communion dress and the other children who died long ago in Oregon, and the girls that he knew Eric Poole had killed here in New England.

"Right," he said. "It's all over." *Maybe I can sleep again.*

But that night he was sleepless as usual, tossing and turning, finally snatching a bit of oblivion before waking to find dawn turning the room to pewter. He knew that it was not all over, would never end. Like the phantom pain that remains after a leg is amputated.

He lit a cigarette, and waited for another day to begin.

In the cell, in the dark, the clatter and the clamour of the jail muffled at last, his thoughts were sharper than ever, and images erupted in his mind like fragments in a kaleidoscope.

Sometimes the images were of his dark girls, flashing eyes, tumbling black hair, always the hair, and his tender invasion of the places where he found tenderness in return.

There were times when he could not summon the girls but other images came: the old cop as he thrust his way out of the bushes. *Still the monster, aren't you, Eric?* He pulled the blanket up to his chin, a chill rattling his bones despite the warmth of the cell. What did the old cop know about monsters? He was tired of the old lieutenant, did not want to think about him any more.

He also did not want to think about his mother, but she emerged in his mind now and then, her long black hair tumbling over him and the odd shape of her mouth as he had last seen her.

He lay still, waiting for sleep to arrive, for the images to fade, wanting only the oblivion that sleep could summon.

But before the oblivion there came the girl. Spinning around in that motel room like a little girl dressed up in her mother's clothes. That silly white hat. And the worst image of all, the one he dreaded but could not prevent: the way she clung to him at the last moment in the waters of the lake: *Love me, Eric.*

Eric touched his cheek, finding moisture there—was this what crying was like?

Later, in the deepest heart of the night, the monster also cried.